BENTON PUBLIC LIBRARY
3 1126 00585 488
W9-BLK-274

Praise for *Things You Can't Say*

"A touching and believable story about the ways worries feed on each other, the difference that honesty makes to kids, and how much emotional growth a child Drew's age can experience in just a few weeks." *—Publishers Weekly*

"A thoughtful examination of the slow, uneven recovery that follows a devastating loss." *—Kirkus Reviews*

"A sensitive exploration of suicide, forgiveness, and the difficulty of navigating friendships." *—Booklist*

"Bishop's emotional novel may provide a way for readers whose lives have been impacted by suicide to navigate a complex topic and will appeal to those who appreciate tales of trauma and healing." *—SLJ*

"With a deft, sympathetic hand, Bishop relates Drew's struggles to define his own identity while coming to terms with the man his father was." *—BCCB*

Also by Jenn Bishop

The Distance to Home

14 Hollow Road

Things You Can't Say

WHERE WE USED TO ROAM

BY JENN BISHOP

ALADDIN
NEW YORK LONDON
TORONTO SYDNEY
NEW DELHI

This book is a work of fiction. Any references to historical events, real people, or real places are used fictitiously. Other names, characters, places, and events are products of the author's imagination, and any resemblance to actual events or places or persons, living or dead, is entirely coincidental.

ALADDIN
An imprint of Simon & Schuster Children's Publishing Division
1230 Avenue of the Americas, New York, New York 10020
First Aladdin hardcover edition March 2021

Book designed by Tiara Iandiorio
The text of this book was set in Adobe Caslon Pro.
Manufactured in the United States of America 0221 FFG
2 4 6 8 10 9 7 5 3 1
Library of Congress Cataloging-in-Publication Data
Names: Bishop, Jenn, author.
Title: Where we used to roam / by Jenn Bishop.
Description: First Aladdin hardcover edition. | New York : Aladdin, 2021. | Audience: Ages 8 to 12. | Summary: Living near Boston, sixth-grader Emma tries to hide from family problems and changing friendships by spending the summer in Wyoming.
Identifiers: LCCN 2020051864 (print) | LCCN 2020051865 (eBook)
ISBN 9781534457294 (hardcover) | ISBN 9781534457317 (eBook)
Subjects: CYAC: Friendship—Fiction. | Family problems—Fiction.
Brothers and sisters—Fiction.
Classification: LCC PZ7.1.B55 Wh 2021 (print) | LCC PZ7.1.B55 (eBook)
DDC [Fic]—dc23
LC record available at https://lccn.loc.gov/2020051864
LC eBook record available at https://lccn.loc.gov/2020051865

For everyone who's a little lost
and looking for their herd

It could be an adventure. That's what Mom told me not even a week ago. But as I stare out the tiny smudged window at the airline worker below as he tosses suitcase after suitcase on the conveyor belt headed for my airplane, I only feel like I'm running away. From what's happening with my brother. From what I did to Becca. From everything.

And not the kind of running away we did as little kids, where you pack your backpack with your favorite snacks, a sweatshirt, and a stuffed animal before hiding out in a neighbor's yard, but the real kind. Putting two thousand miles between yourself and everything and everyone you know.

A tall guy who can't be much older than Austin, with dark brown skin, gentle eyes, and a Boston

College men's basketball sweatshirt, slides into the seat next to me. "Sorry," he says, with no choice but to spread his legs open, his knee knocking into mine. "They were all out of exit-row seats."

I pivot my legs toward the window and out of his way. "No worries," I say. "Do you play?" I gesture to his sweatshirt.

"Yeah," he says. "Forward. You?"

I can't help but laugh at the suggestion. "No, but my brother, Austin, he . . ." *Used to.* The words slip out of my grasp. He will again, I tell myself. Thirty days on Cape Cod is going to fix him. It has to.

"Cool, cool," he says before slipping red headphones over his ears.

Soon, the plane is filled up. All these people headed to Denver or even farther away. Like me. Except, probably not like me. I bet they're on vacation or traveling for business. Or going home for the summer now that all the colleges around Boston have let out.

When it's time for takeoff, I shut my eyes tight, but this time when I close them, all I see is my brother in the upstairs hallway. Austin, with his hand in a fist. How mad he looked, but not at me—at himself.

I don't like that Austin, can't look at that version of him anymore. I open my eyes and peer out the window as the plane dips to the left and the deep blue water of the Atlantic Ocean glimmers in the sun. I reach down, loosen the straps on my Birkenstocks, and rest my feet on my backpack. The vibrations from the engine travel up through my whole body, like they're trying to soothe me.

The plane levels off, and we head west over the city. The skyscrapers downtown suddenly don't seem so tall. Down below, I spy the green lawn of Boston Common, the muddy water of the Charles, the stone buildings on the Harvard campus.

Becca must be down there somewhere, at the camp she goes to every summer with her fellow geniuses. All the other summers, she'd complain, wishing I could accompany her. But this summer?

No, this summer I'm sure she's glad to be away from me and everyone else from our school. Happy for a fresh start after how I ruined her life.

I rummage through my backpack for my sketchbook, flip it open to a clean page, and wipe my sweaty palms on my lap before uncapping my pen.

Dear Becca, I write, before stopping to stare out the window again. Everything's so small, like a dollhouse world. Tiny Matchbox cars zipping down the Mass Pike. From up here you can't see the people inside. From up here it looks perfect.

That's how my life used to be. I didn't realize it until now—didn't have anything else to compare it to—but it was.

I close my eyes again, but now all I see is that look on Becca's face, almost like I'd slapped her. It was my chance to apologize, to try to make things right, but all I did was make things worse. Me and my big mouth. Guess all that time hanging out with Kennedy finally wore off on me.

I press my pen to the paper. *I'm sorr—*

Some turbulence sends the pen jumping across the page, leaving a huge scribble behind. I close the notebook, put the cap back on the pen. I can write to her later. I have the whole flight. The whole summer, really.

Two months to figure out how to fix the mess I made.

SEVEN MONTHS EARLIER

CHAPTER ONE

Maybe everything could have been different if Ms. Patel—sorry, Nisha—had never approached me in art class. Not that any of what happened after is her fault. It's just that something—someone—had to be the first domino to fall. The one that sent all the others toppling. And if I think back, it was that moment that set it all into motion.

At least as far as Becca was concerned.

It was seventh period, the last class of the day before Thanksgiving break. But you wouldn't have been able to tell from peeking into the art room on that gray day. Ms. Patel always had music playing in her room—a mix of her own CDs and student iPhones plugged into her speaker system.

We'd rotated into art only a few weeks earlier with

the start of second quarter, so I still didn't know her that well, but already I liked her a whole lot more than Mr. Morris, who we'd had for health last quarter. Seemed like his job was mostly to scare us away from trying drugs.

I was half listening to the music, some kind of punk mix that my brother would probably be into, while I worked on my portrait drawing. Instead of randomly pairing us with other students in the class—the definition of awkward—Ms. Patel asked us to bring in a photograph of a family member or a loved one. "No celebrities," she'd said when Teagan Washington tried to pass off a picture of Timothée Chalamet as a "distant cousin."

The one I'd been bringing to life the past few classes was a photo of my brother. A snapshot Dad had taken at one of Austin's football practices this summer. Austin and his teammates were goofing off on the sidelines. It was one of those rare pictures that truly looks like the person. Every time I look at a photo of myself, it never quite matches up to the *me* I see in the mirror. The me I'm used to. And maybe mirror *me* isn't real me after all. But still.

I was shading in the laugh lines around Austin's eyes when Ms. Patel stopped behind me. Her curly black hair was always up in a messy bun, and she had the kind of funky plastic glasses you'd expect on an artist. Like she'd picked them out because she wanted to look interesting, rather than pretty.

"Nice work, Emma," she said. "That your older brother?"

I nodded, not stopping working just because she was there. There were only a few minutes left before the bell would ring, and I wanted to finish his eyes.

"I can see the resemblance." She picked up the photograph. Her fingers were flecked with paint—metallic blue and burnt umber.

"Really?" I set my pencil down.

"Absolutely. It's all about the composition—how your nose, eyes, and mouth relate to each other. The exact same proportions."

My heart sank a little. It wasn't like I wanted my art teacher to tell me I was beautiful or something. That would be weird. And it's not like I think my own brother is attractive. Also weird. But there are some things you kind of figure out from living in the world, from seeing how people react to other people. Austin was one of those shiny people. The kind everyone paid attention to when he walked into a room. Mom and Dad, too.

But me? No one had ever really noticed *me* that way. I blended in with the scenery.

"You know," Ms. Patel said, setting the photo back down, "we're always welcoming new folks to art club. You should come sometime and see what it's like."

"Even in the middle of the school year?"

"Especially in the middle of the school year. So much of middle school is new, and it can take a little while to find your place. Have you taken art classes before? Private lessons?"

"Nope," I said. Though we live in the kind of Boston suburb where everyone's been taking lessons in something—or five somethings—since they were in diapers, Mom and Dad were never super into that with me and Austin. Between Dad's job as a meteorologist at the TV station and Mom buying Happy Feet when I started kindergarten, there wasn't anyone left to ferry us around in the afternoons. Austin had his teammates' parents to take him to sports practices, and me? When I wasn't over at the Grossmans' house with my best friend, Becca, my after-school activity was hiding out in Mom's office in the back of the running store. Drawing in my notebook, surrounded by boxes of the latest New Balance and Asics.

"You're quite talented for being self-taught," Ms. Patel said as the bell rang. "I hope you'll consider coming, Emma. And not that I need to seal the deal, but I do provide brownies."

My mouth watered. "Maybe," I said with a smile, not wanting to give away how much she'd already sold me on it. "Have a nice Thanksgiving!" I slipped my drawing into my folder.

"You too, Emma. Hope to see you Tuesday!"

After stopping by my locker, I met Becca outside the school, by that one maple tree where we always met to walk home together. She was so glued to the book she was reading, she didn't even notice me at first.

"Becca?" I said finally.

"Sorry!" She tucked in her bookmark. "Mrs. Hanson saved it for me. It doesn't come out till next Tuesday, but she said so long as I don't tell anyone."

"Even me?" I said as we began our walk home.

"Well, you know! You don't really care about books."

Ouch. She wasn't wrong. It's not like I never read, but if you were going to compare me to Becca, it was no contest. No one at our middle school read more than Becca Grossman. Not even Mrs. Hanson, the middle school librarian. And that's saying a lot because I'm pretty sure I overheard Mrs. Hanson saying she read more than three hundred books in a single year.

"Why is this one so special?" I asked.

"It's the fifth and final one in the series." Becca pouted. "Though, maybe if us fans clamor enough, we can get the author to put out a novella or something. It's happened before! I know what I'm doing over break." She hugged the book to her chest.

"Or *tonight*, if I know you."

"But then I'll probably reread it a few times. Put some stickies on my favorite scenes."

"We can still go to the movies though, right?"

"Definitely," Becca said as she adjusted her glasses. "I need to give my eyes a break sometime."

"So," I said, shoving my hands in my pockets. "I think I might check out art club next week."

"Art club?" Becca wrinkled her nose.

“What’s so wrong with art club?”

“The kind of people who do art club,” Becca said, as if it were a certified fact that the people who do art club are weirdos.

I got this strange feeling in my stomach then. Did my wanting to do it mean she felt that way about me, too? Just a little?

“But I don’t know who does art club,” I said. “Not for sure. I haven’t even gone yet.”

“You should’ve signed up for Battle of the Books back in September. But hey, you could still do Forensics with me! That doesn’t start for a few more weeks.”

I *had* been interested in Forensics. But that was before I realized it wasn’t like *CSI* at all. Once I learned it was about giving speeches, no thanks!

When we first visited the middle school as fifth graders back in the spring, I’d been so excited. There were tons more after-school activities than we had in elementary, and since the middle school was walking distance from my house, it didn’t matter anymore that no one was around to drive me. Becca and I, we could just walk home.

But here we were, more than a quarter into the

school year, and I hadn't signed up for anything. It was easier for Austin. When you do sports, it's all figured out for you. Fall was for football, then he had basketball all winter, and track in the spring. I promised Mom I'd *try* spring track, but right now spring felt a long way away. And Becca did a million activities. I needed something.

"I don't know," I said.

"What about math club? You're good at math."

She wasn't wrong. It was my best subject. Well, after art. I'd just never had a chance to do art for a grade. Still, I wasn't nearly as good at math as Becca, who was taking it at the *high school.*

"Maybe," I said as we waited at a crosswalk. But it was entirely different from the "maybe" I'd given Ms. Patel just fifteen minutes ago.

If I wanted to do something, why did it matter whether or not Becca was on board?

CHAPTER TWO

It was my brother who spotted the shadow boxes first. Just over two years ago, when the four of us went to Chicago when my mom ran the marathon. Dad was never good at standing around quietly and looking at stuff, so Austin was always the one who'd go with me to museums.

We'd taken selfies at the Bean and left Dad to explore Millennium Park while Austin and I checked out the Art Institute.

"You ever hear of this guy, Em? Joseph Cornell?" Austin had stopped in front of a box on the wall. It reminded me of the dioramas we made for school projects sometimes, except this one was different. For one, it wasn't cardboard. It had a glass front and wooden sides, and in the back was a piece of wood with a hole cut out, the kind of thing you might peek through. Sitting on the bottom of the box was a small globe, a little blue cube, and a red bead. "Guess he was a collector, too."

The Art Institute had dozens of these shadow boxes by Joseph Cornell. Some with layers of text, almost like decoupage. Several with birds and owls. One with a creepy naked doll. I was immediately obsessed with them. I couldn't get over how the way he'd arranged these objects in a box seemed to tell a story. Or give you a feeling. It was so much more than just some random stuff in a box. And at the same time, it was exactly that.

Ever since I was little I'd held on to things. Mom wasn't one of those minimalist moms, and she was never really strict about what Austin and I did with our bedrooms. Beneath my bed and in my closet were boxes of stuff I'd saved. When we got back home from Chicago, I made my first-ever shadow box with some of my treasures from when I was little. A lovey that had made a few too many trips through the washing machine and dryer. One of those trinkets I'd begged Dad for a quarter to buy at the grocery store—a miniature plastic person.

And three shiny pennies. According to Dad, Grandpa Bill had let me go through his wallet when I was little and I had asked him, 100 percent serious, if when he was very, very old and about to die, I could have the three shiny pennies. They'd all had a good laugh and Grandpa Bill gave them to me that day.

I glued them to the back of the box, the way I'd noticed Joseph Cornell did in some of his boxes, and laid out the other items on the bottom.

Dad helped me hang the shadow box on the wall in my bedroom like it was in a museum. "My very own Joseph Cornell," I'd said.

Dad corrected me. "Your very first Emma O'Malley. You never know, Em. This could be worth something one day."

I laughed him off. Probably blushed, too. But ever since, when I think of that moment and how my dad took me seriously, I realize how lucky I am. There aren't a whole lot of other kids in my school whose parents would be okay with them wanting to be an artist. At least, I don't think. No, most people's parents want them to be doctors or lawyers, or to work in tech. Even though Becca loves reading more than life itself, she already knows she wants to be a doctor when she grows up, like her parents.

The Saturday after Thanksgiving, I was up late, working on my latest shadow box. A playlist was on softly in the background.

When she was doing the dishes after the big meal, Mom accidentally dropped one of her favorite plates, a delicate crystal one she'd inherited from her great-grandmother, and it shattered into dozens of pieces. She was about to throw it away when I asked if I could have it for one of my boxes. "So long as you're careful and don't cut yourself," she'd said with a smile. "I mean it. No trips to the ER for your art, please."

Mom's birthday was in January, and I figured I could make a box for her, though I still hadn't decided what exactly would go in it besides the mosaic background I'd been imagining, made out of the fragmented glass.

Downstairs, I could hear the front door close. Austin had just come home.

I peeked my head out the door as he passed my room.

Austin jumped. "You scared the crap out of me, Em. Why are you still up? It's one in the morning."

Was it really that late? "I was working on a box." I followed him into his room. He grabbed a sweatshirt that had been dumped on his desk and kicked off his sneakers. The air around him smelled funny, sort of like a skunk.

"What do you think this is, a sleepover?" He laughed, settling down on his bed and nestling his head into a pile of pillows. Mom didn't make either of our beds anymore—that was up to us after third grade—which meant Austin's bed was never, ever made unless his girlfriend, Savannah, was coming over.

"I'll leave in a minute." I sat down at the edge of his bcd. "Was it fun?"

"Hmmm. Are parties fun? Let's see . . ."

"Stop it!" I giggled. "I've never been to a high school party. Remember?"

"Yeah, yeah, yeah. But someday you will."

"I don't know," I said. I couldn't imagine me or Becca ever going to one of those parties Austin goes to on the weekends, when his friends' parents are out of town.

"You just need to find your people," he said, his head settling further into the pillows. From that angle, it looked like he had three chins. No, maybe four?

"My people?" I asked as Austin's eyes started to close.

His eyelids fluttered open and he shifted upright. "Yeah, Em. Your people. You know, most of my friends now, I didn't know them in elementary school. God, in elementary school I was friends with Brian Fitzgibbons! Ol' Fitzy! It takes a while to find your true friends. The ones who *really* get you. Your herd." I glanced up at the Modest Mouse poster above Austin's bed, the one with the ginormous buffalo. "Some people don't find them till college, which must suck, but a lot of people, they find them in middle school or high school. There's tons of people out there, Em. You just gotta look."

In my head, all I could see was Becca wrinkling her nose at the idea of art club. But what if Austin was right? What if that was where I met *my* people? Found my herd. To be fair, my brother, a high school junior, had a whole lot more expertise when it came to making friends than Becca or I ever did. Maybe he was right.

"Do you think . . . ?"

"I do."

"No!" I laughed. "I wasn't done asking the question—"

"Well, speed it up, Em. It's one in the morning and some of us need our beauty rest."

I rolled my eyes. "Do you think I should join the art club?"

"How are you not *already* in art club, Em?"

I shrugged. "Becca wasn't into it. . . ."

"Oh, I'm sorry, since when does Becca call all the shots?"

I had no answer for him.

"Em, you've got to do some stuff without Becca sometimes! No shade to Becca, but just because she doesn't want to do something doesn't mean *you* can't. What if the artsy weirdos are your people? Spoiler alert: they probably are. I mean, you're up in the middle of the night doing art for fun! Why should you have to miss out on that because it's not Becca's jam? You're your own person, Em. Promise." He lay back down on his bed and mumbled, "I think that was a pretty good motivational speech."

"You know I can hear you, right?"

"It's been a long night. The border between

thoughts and speech is a little hazy." He closed his eyes again, and I had a feeling this time it was for good.

"Don't fall asleep in your clothes."

"Okay, *Mom*." His eyes stayed closed. His chest rose and fell with each breath, and I started to wonder if he might really fall asleep like that.

"Hey, Austin?"

"Yeah," he murmured.

"Thank you."

"Anytime, Em."

I slid off his bed and tiptoed out of the room, shutting off the overhead light on my way out.

"Night, Austin," I whispered, closing his door gently behind me.

CHAPTER THREE

You're your own person, Em. Promise. My brother's words echoed in my head the following Tuesday as I hung around my locker a few extra minutes before going upstairs to the art room.

I didn't know why I was nervous. It wasn't like Ms. Patel was scary. And in any case, no matter how awkward it was to go to a club where I didn't know a soul, at least I was going to get a homemade brownie out of it.

Right. A brownie! Mmm. There was my motivation.

When I got upstairs, the early-afternoon light was streaming through the big windows of the art room. The eighth graders, I think, had made stained glass, and the very best ones—and okay, maybe some of the very worst, too—were hung over the window so that fragments of blue and red and green light glittered onto the tables below.

"So glad you decided to come." Ms. Patel turned from the easel where she was working on a painting in all black and white. It was abstract, and still at an early stage, so I couldn't tell what she was going for. "Brownies, as promised, are out on the table. I hope you like double chocolate chip."

"Who doesn't?" I replied.

"Exactly," she said. "Oh, and once the bell rings for the day, I am done being Ms. Patel. Call me Nisha, okay?"

I was pretty sure I could never call a teacher by a first name even if I tried, but I said, "Sure," anyway, and made my way over to the brownies.

Besides Ms. Patel—sorry, Nisha—no one else had really gotten started on anything yet. The other students were clustered around the brownies. Two eighth graders I knew from when we had to take the bus back in elementary school, Aisha Simmons and Danica St. Clair, and two girls I didn't recognize. One of them was Asian, with long super straight black hair and wearing a hat with a fox head. The other was tall and white, with shoulder-length blond hair that had a chunk dyed hot pink.

"Hey," Fox Hat said as I reached in for a brownie. "You new?"

"Yeah," I said. "Emma. I'm in sixth grade."

"Us too!" she said. "I'm Lucy and this is Kennedy."

"We just transferred this year from Comey Valley Charter," Kennedy said. She had a gap between her front teeth, just wide enough that you could slip a quarter between them. "Do you want to sit with us?"

"Sure," I said, following them over to a table by the window. "Have you been coming since the beginning of the school year?"

Kennedy nodded. "Our parents said we had to do something after school to meet people, but there aren't a whole lot of sixth graders in art club."

"Except Henry." Lucy pointed to a boy I hadn't noticed, in the corner. He was dressed in all black and wearing headphones while making something out of clay.

"Right. Yeah. And no." Kennedy laughed. "Now we can tell them we met you! See, we *are* meeting people. And we're so good at it, right? Not at all creepy." She opened her eyes extra wide and reached over, grabbing Lucy's shoulders.

"You see what I have to deal with," Lucy deadpanned.

Kennedy seemed like a lot, that was for sure, but not in a bad way. She reminded me a little of my cousin Baxter when he had too much caffeine. While Lucy excused herself to go grab her project, Kennedy pulled out a notebook from her backpack. "I'll show you mine if you'll show me yours."

I reached into my backpack, suddenly hesitant. I'd never shown my notebook to anyone, not even Becca.

"Oh, come on, it can't be weirder than this kid Kyle back at Comey. Kyle drew nutso pictures of murdering people. And then he mysteriously stopped coming to school one day. Now that I think about it, what *did* happen to him?" She tapped her chin and raised one eyebrow.

When Lucy returned, I noticed her slip-on sneakers had sloths on them. She set down a collage made from the teeny-tiniest magazine clippings. It wasn't completed enough for me to see where she was going with it, but I was intrigued. "Yeah, Kyle was super shady," Lucy said.

"Okay, fine." I traded notebooks with Kennedy. "But it won't make sense if I don't—"

"One, two, three—oh, whoa!"

I chewed on my lip as Kennedy flipped through the pages. The first quarter of the notebook was an inventory of the shoeboxes under my bed. The pages after were sketches, ideas of what I could bring to life with all those pieces.

"Do you make these boxes from scratch?" Lucy asked, peering over Kennedy's shoulder.

"My dad has a lot of leftover wood in the garage. And sometimes I find old ones at the Take It or Leave It."

I felt like a jerk all of a sudden, looking over my own stuff when I should have been looking at Kennedy's art. I flipped open her notebook. Inked inside were manga sketches. Some of them were characters I recognized, but others were completely original. Their eyes, wide and detailed, their mouths so animated and expressive. A girl with big black boots, one of them raised like she was about to kick someone's butt. "These are incredible."

"They're all right," Kennedy said. If I knew her better, I'd say she was being modest, but I still didn't know her that well. "Your boxes . . . are any of them done?"

"Yeah," I said, thinking of the growing gallery on my bedroom wall. Seven, not counting the one I'd just started for my mom.

My best was probably the one that came in first in mixed media at the town art show this summer. Not exactly a major accomplishment given that I'm too young for the teen category, but still. It had a shattered window with a baseball and a broken teacup resting at the bottom. Dad asked if it could be "on loan" for the year, so like a real collector, I was lending it to him. It was up on the wall in his office at NBC Boston.

"I hope we can see one sometime," Kennedy said.

"Yeah," Lucy chimed in. "Those are way cool. I've never seen anything like them before."

"Thanks," I said. For a second I imagined Austin watching us. *What did I tell you? Your big brother knows everything.*

Kennedy handed my notebook back carefully, like she got that it was a treasured object. Hers probably was too. I passed it back, and for the next hour and a half, until the late buses lined up outside, we drew.

Well, Kennedy drew. I'd packed some magazines to look through for my mom's shadow box. My hope was to find something delicate and beautiful to adhere to the inside of the glass, but I still wasn't sure what. Sometimes the best parts were the images I stumbled upon by chance. Lucy cut and glued, humming along with the music. When Kennedy got stuck or frustrated, she would color on her nails with markers.

"So, why did you transfer?" I asked.

Lucy and Kennedy looked at each other like they were trying to decide who should answer, and then Kennedy started talking. I had the feeling this was how it always was with the two of them.

"One of my moms changed jobs," Kennedy said. "And her new commute made it tricky to do drop-off and pickup at the charter school."

"Gotcha," I said.

"And then Lucy"—Kennedy uncapped a brown marker—"couldn't imagine life without me, so she decided to transfer, too." She quickly drew a little squirrel on Lucy's biceps.

"You like animals, huh?" I said, thinking about Lucy's fox hat, sloth sneakers, and now this.

"Yeah, she—" Kennedy started to say something, but then Lucy cut her off.

"She asked *me*." Lucy ignored Kennedy sticking out her tongue. "When I grow up I either want to be a vet or work in the music industry. Like in Nashville or LA or New York City."

"Those are pretty different things," I said. "And places."

Lucy shrugged. "What do you want to be when you grow up?"

Was it weird that I didn't know yet? All I knew was it wasn't going to be something like what Mom and Dad did. Every day, surrounded by so many people, having to be *on* all the time. "I'm not sure," I said.

Kennedy eyed my arm. "My tattooing urge has not been quenched."

"Okay, fine." I took an arm out of my hoodie and extended it toward her.

The marker tickled my skin, and it was hard to hold my arm straight without giggling. At first I couldn't tell what she was drawing, but as she continued it became clear.

"It's you!" Kennedy let my arm drop. "And okay, I

hope your parents don't get mad, but these markers are not super washable. . . ."

"They won't care." I twisted my forearm for a better look at my manga self. She'd gotten everything right. My long ponytail, my black-and-white-checked leggings, my huge hoodie, my New Balance. And my sketchbook, clutched to my chest.

She'd seen me. *Me.*

CHAPTER FOUR

The following day at school, I found Kennedy and Lucy in the cafeteria. Turned out, we'd all had fourth-period lunch the whole time and never even knew. Which was good news for me, since Becca had fifth-period lunch, and I'd been sitting with a bunch of girls from my ELA class who were nice, sure, but they spent most of lunch talking about which jeans made their butts look good. As Austin said, they weren't exactly my people. But the more time I spent with Lucy and Kennedy, I was starting to think they were. And I wanted Becca to meet them, so I invited them to my brother's football game that Saturday. The high school team was in the state finals, which was a pretty big deal. Or at least a big deal to people who care about football.

"I think you'll like them," I told Becca Friday morning on our walk to school. "Kennedy's kind of loud, but she's funny. And Lucy can be really quiet, but then she'll just slay you with something. Like the other day at lunch, you should've seen her impression of this contestant from *The Voice*. She could be on *SNL* someday."

"Do they like football?" Becca asked.

"Do *we*?"

Becca laughed. "Good point." We'd been tagging along with my parents to Austin's games ever since he was on JV. And sure, neither of us would ever be able to explain all the rules of football, but we could tell when a touchdown happened. And honestly, that was really all that mattered. When everyone around us cheered, we cheered too. When everyone around us was bummed, we were bummed.

And when everyone around us lost their minds because of something amazing that happened on the field, that was when we lived it up. My arms would turn into confetti rockets. Pretend, obviously. And Becca would mime amazement at all of the confetti blasting out of my arms.

It was a whole thing.

Kennedy and Lucy were getting a ride from Lucy's stepdad, who was meeting up with some old friends at the game. Becca rode with us.

"Did I tell you about Stoughton's linebacker?" Dad said as we idled in traffic, heading onto the Pike. "Three hundred pounds."

Even though she was in the front seat, I could hear Mom grit her teeth. "I'd rather you didn't."

For the past few years, Mom had been reading studies about the long-term damage from concussions and trying to convince Austin to switch to cross-country. Dad said it was pointless—you couldn't take football away from Austin *now*—and he'd remind Mom that Austin wasn't good enough or big enough to play in college anyway. Plus, Dad had played football in high school too, and his brain was perfectly fine. Mom said that was "debatable."

The twenty minutes to the stadium might've felt like forever with Mom and Dad getting testy, but having Becca in the back always saved me.

Ever since we were little, we'd been playing the same game on long car rides. Especially when we went to the

Cape. We'd make up stories about the people in the cars that we passed or that passed us, trying to top each other.

A Mercedes-Benz station wagon pulled up alongside us. The driver's shoulder-length gray hair was blown out, and she had on huge black sunglasses.

"She's going to the funeral of her secret lover. They'd just gotten back together after twenty years apart when he died unexpectedly," I said.

"How'd he die?" Becca asked.

"Choking to death on a hot dog."

Becca snorted. "Glamorous."

"It was an across-the-tracks love affair. He was a hot dog vendor at Fenway."

"How tragic," she said playfully, glancing out her window as we passed a beat-up Mazda pickup. "Ooh! That's a good one! He is a part-time geophysicist. Full-time serial killer."

"But is he going to work?" I asked. "Or on the hunt for his next victim?"

"Both!" Becca was cracking herself up. Me too. I was starting to realize I should've peed before we'd left the house.

"This game's kind of morbid, no?" Mom asked.

"It's fun, though," I said. "And it's just pretend."

"Sorry, Mrs. O'Malley. We can stop if it's bothering you."

"Maybe tone it down a tiny notch? Perhaps I'm a little more squeamish than your parents."

She definitely was. I'm pretty sure anyone was. Being surgeons, Becca's parents had been deep into all that gross body stuff for so long it wasn't even gross anymore. Well, to them. One time I was at their house for dinner and her dad told us this story about how one of his patients hadn't pooped for twenty-six days. I'd like to unhear that one, actually.

"Ooh! Great one coming up on the right," Mom said. A Peter Pan bus had broken down on the shoulder.

Becca and I locked eyes. "Tag team!" We took turns concocting an elaborate story about how the bus driver had spent his whole life searching the streets of Boston for his long-lost love, only to find her today. Unfortunately for both of them, she was now trapped in the bus bathroom and it was about to explode.

Lucy and Kennedy were waiting for us at the stadium's main gate. Kennedy had dyed her streak bright green for the occasion—our high school's colors were green and yellow. She and Lucy had already written *GHS* on their cheeks with green and yellow face crayons.

"Luce! Ken! You're here!" I squealed.

"Are. You. Ready. For. Some. Football?" Lucy deadpanned before breaking into a smile. "Just kidding," she said. "It's like a rite of passage. At least, that's what my dad said. Everyone should go to one high school football game in their life, right?"

"One." Kennedy held up her pointer finger. "One."

Becca coughed.

"Oh, right! Sorry. I'm bad at this. So, Kennedy, Lucy, this is my friend Becca. Becca, this is Kennedy. And this is Lucy." For some reason I was gesturing wildly with my hands like I was on an infomercial, trying to sell Becca on all the features of my exciting new product.

"Cool," Becca said. "Should we go find some seats?"

"Right! Right, right, right. Wouldn't want to miss one moment of the football! Do they do cheers?" Kennedy asked. "I love me a good cheer."

"We can teach you the cheers," I said.

We ended up sitting a few rows back from my

parents, who were sitting with all the other players' parents. I let Kennedy and Lucy head down our row first, so I'd be right in the middle in between them and Becca.

Kennedy pulled some face crayons out of her coat pocket. "Want me to do yours?" she asked me and Becca.

"Sure," I said right away, pointing to my left cheek. "Can you write number twenty-two here? That's Austin's number." When she finished, Lucy took a picture on her phone so I could see.

"Becca?" Kennedy asked.

Becca shook her head. "No thanks. I have sensitive skin."

Sensitive skin? Since when? We'd been getting our faces painted since we were little kids. At town festivals, ball games, the zoo. I couldn't remember a time when Becca had *ever* said no to face paint. But before I had a chance to ask, the loudspeakers began playing music and we were all on our feet, bouncing in the stands.

Right out of the gate, our high school's team, the Tigers, scored a touchdown. My arms were doing their confetti rocket thing, but instead of basking in all of the confetti that had miraculously shot out of my arms, Becca was just standing there, clapping politely. Eventually I had to stop doing it. It didn't work the same without Becca playing along. I just looked like a weirdo.

"What were you doing there?" Lucy asked once the crowds quieted down. "With your arms."

I gave her some of the backstory. "It doesn't really work with just one person, I guess."

"Well, now that we know what's going on, *we* can do it. Next time!" She turned to Kennedy and filled her in. Becca had her phone out, taking some pictures of the action down on the field where Austin was.

I cupped my hands around my mouth. "Let's go, Tigers! Let's do this!"

Ten minutes later, when GHS scored their next touchdown, we were on our feet again. I launched my confetti rockets in the direction of Kennedy and Lucy. They basked in the make-believe shower of confetti.

Kennedy took it to the next level, catching imaginary confetti in her mouth like it was snowflakes. Chomp. Chomp. Chomp!

"That was *our* thing," Becca said, so quietly I wasn't sure I heard her right.

"What?" I asked, turning toward her.

"Nothing." She took her seat.

I wanted to say something else, but there really wasn't time at a football game to have a whole conversation. Especially at the state finals.

"Let's go, Tigers, let's go!" Kennedy shouted.

"Yeah, Tigers!" I strained, trying to find my brother down on the field.

Austin was winding up to throw when a defender from the other team slammed into him from behind. That fast, my brother went down.

Lucy grabbed my shoulder. "Is he okay?"

"Yeah, sure. He gets hit all the time." I glanced over at Becca for confirmation that this was a normal part of a football game, but Becca's jaw had tightened. Her gaze was fixed on the field. On my brother.

"No, Em. I'm serious," Lucy said. "He's not getting up."

Down below, a ref blew a whistle. One of the trainers rushed onto the field, and another jogged out after him. The whole stadium hushed, everyone frozen in place. Except for the two people who stood up at the same time, pushing their way out of the row and down to field level. My parents.

"I'd better go with them." I got up, my legs suddenly wobbly. My brother was still down on the ground with trainers hovering over him.

"I'm coming with you," Becca said.

"Us too," Lucy added.

I waved them all off, but Becca followed anyway. I scooted down our row, making my way to the aisle, and ran down the steps, nearly tripping on the metal bleachers. My hands balled into fists inside the sleeves of Austin's old football sweatshirt, the one I wore for all his games. The one I always thought brought good luck.

So much for that.

All I could think about was what Dad said in the car. *Three hundred pounds.* Three hundred pounds of solid muscle, slamming into my brother. Austin was big and strong, but he wasn't *that* big, not *that* strong. I wanted to be on the field, right there next to him, holding his hand. Even if he didn't want me to.

By the time Becca and I were a few yards away

from my parents, down at the sidelines, Austin was finally sitting up, but the trainers were still squatting, huddled around him. Murmurs spread through the crowd. The knot in my stomach loosened the tiniest bit.

"Mom!" I croaked. And then I was right beside her as she hugged me close.

One of the trainers had his hand on Austin's arm, trying to lift it, but not getting very far before Austin winced. Was something wrong with his shoulder? Was it broken? Can you break a shoulder?

Austin always talked away his aches and pains, said they were no big deal. But he cursed, his face twisting in pain, as one of the trainers popped his shoulder back into place. I couldn't stop wincing, just watching all of it. Once the shoulder was in, though, his face calmed down, and that helped me calm down too. So did having Becca beside me. She was as quiet as I was, but that was okay. Sometimes there's no right thing to say. Just being there is enough.

Soon Austin was up, walking off the field, the crowd cheering for him. The second-string quarterback ran out onto the field, a big smile on his face.

Of course, this meant something different for him. He was going to get in the game now.

"Em." When I turned around, they were right there too. Lucy, tugging at the little paws dangling from her fox hat. Kennedy, beside her, biting her lip.

"He's going to be okay," I told them, even though I didn't know for sure.

CHAPTER FIVE

One of the team trainers offered to come with us to the emergency room at Mount Auburn Hospital, but Mom and Dad insisted they could take care of things from here, thank you.

Becca's Bubbe met us at the hospital to take her home. Becca didn't want to leave us, but her Bubbe insisted there was nothing she could do to help. They'd offered to let me stay the night at Becca's, but I wanted to be here with my family.

Austin kept saying he was fine, he just needed a couple of Advil and some ice, that's all the doctors were going to do anyway, but Mom said no way and Dad agreed.

We'd been sitting for half an hour and still nobody had called Austin's name. Mom flipped through an old *Runner's World* she'd brought in from the car, too fast to be reading any of the articles. Dad was on his phone, researching shoulder dislocations.

Austin's phone vibrated and dinged as friends sent updates from the game. The score had tightened since we left.

I'd been in an emergency room only once before, two years ago, when Dad was in Florida covering a hurricane. Austin had been helping Mom make dinner when he cut his thumb on one of the sharp knives. He ended up needing only two stitches, but that was hard to tell because Mom had wrapped his hand up real good with a kitchen towel.

It felt scary that time, but I think only because Dad was so far away. Mom had assured me that Austin was going to be fine. These things happen all the time. Just a little accident. Nothing to get too bent out of shape over.

But no one was saying that now, and I couldn't tell if that was because they didn't want to make Austin upset, or because there was still a good chance this could end up okay. I'd watched enough sports with Dad to see that sometimes things could look really bad on the field, but then his favorite player would be back the next weekend.

I didn't know what to think, only that Mom and Dad didn't want to say anything until Austin had seen a doctor, so I kept my questions to myself. All I knew was, Austin seemed pretty much okay. Okay enough to be on his phone. And he wasn't bleeding anywhere, so that had to be good, right?

A TV perched in the corner was running an episode of *Dateline NBC* about some twenty-year-old unsolved murder, but they didn't put the sound on, so it was impossible to follow. It was more interesting to watch the other people who were waiting. A woman in her twenties who was there by herself, her legs crossed, one foot swinging in the air. A man trying to calm a toddler who kept wailing and wailing.

"Noooo!" Austin shouted out of the blue.

"What happened?" I asked.

Austin leaned forward, wincing for a moment. "We lost."

Mom and Dad exchanged a nervous glance.

"I'm so sorry, A," Dad said. "What was the final score?"

"Twenty-four to twenty-two."

"So close," I said.

"God, if I'd still been there, maybe—"

"Austin O'Malley?" A male nurse carrying a clipboard stepped into the waiting room.

Austin slowly stood up. Dad tried to help him, but Austin shooed him off.

"Can I come too?" I asked.

Mom put a hand on my knee as if to hold me in place. "Those ER rooms are tiny, hon. Let's let Dad and Austin go in." She added to my dad, "Holler if you need me. And take good notes, please." They followed the nurse through the closed doors.

When *Dateline* ended and the local news came on, Austin and Dad still hadn't come back out. I couldn't stop yawning. Mom put her arm around me, and I nestled my head onto her shoulder, trying not to look at the strange stains on the carpet and wonder where they'd come from. I must have fallen asleep because the next thing I knew, Mom was talking on her phone.

"Oh, Dee. I don't know. You know kids these days. He's surely thinking there's some quick fix, but nothing I've read online makes me think . . ."

It had to be Delia, her best friend from college who lived in Wyoming. Even though they sometimes didn't see each other in person for a few years, they talked or texted nearly every day.

"I know. You're right. Let the doctors do their work. No WebMD for me. Thanks, Dee. You're the best. Ooh—here they are."

Dad and Austin came out the double doors. Austin's arm was in a sling.

"What did they say?" I asked.

But Austin only shook his head. His eyes looked pink and watery.

"Dad?"

"We'll need to see a specialist to figure out the next steps, E."

I rubbed at my eyes. *Next steps?* "Is he going to be able to play basketball?"

"Emma!" Mom shot me a look, except I didn't get it. What was so wrong with my question? Wasn't that why we were here? To figure this out? To fix Austin?

As we trudged out to the car, a nearly full moon shining down on us, I asked Austin again. "What did the doctor say?" I asked it quietly this time, so Mom and Dad wouldn't hear.

His nostrils flared. "She said I'm screwed, Emma. Jesus! Read the room." A choking sob caught in his throat.

"I'm sorry," I said as the car honked twice from Dad unlocking it with his key fob. I wanted to say something more, anything to make him feel better. But I was afraid if I said the wrong thing again, all I'd do was make him even angrier with me.

When we got home, no one said a word. Not Mom, not Dad. Not Austin.

I was still untying my sneakers when Austin stomped up the stairs, slamming his bedroom door behind him.

I thought maybe Mom or Dad would say something. Tell him to calm down, that everything was going to be okay. But they didn't go up after him.

"Leave him be," Dad whispered as I started up the stairs. "We've all had a long night."

There was a small line of light peeking out beneath Austin's door, but he wasn't making a sound. I hesitated right outside his room. Downstairs, Mom and Dad were talking. Dad wouldn't even know if I went in. I wouldn't ask any dumb questions, not this time. I'd just listen.

I grabbed some scratch paper from my desk and scrawled out a note. *If you change your mind and want to talk, I'll be awake.* Just as I was about to cap my pen, I added, *Sorry about earlier*, and then I rapped lightly on Austin's door and slid him the message.

I waited outside, listening as the floorboards creaked.

A minute later, the paper poked back out beneath the door. *Sorry for blowing up at you*, Austin had written. *This whole thing sucks but I'll live.* He'd drawn a stick figure with a smiley face and a big Band-Aid over its shoulder. For someone who liked looking at art, Austin had always been pretty awful at making it.

I stuck the drawing in one of the boxes under my bed. Maybe Becca was right that time she said my shadow boxes were a long-con cover-up for my hoarding tendencies. Maybe I was a little bit of a hoarder. But at least my brother wasn't still mad at me.

Austin wasn't able to see a specialist for his shoulder until Thursday. When Becca and I got to my house late that afternoon, Mom's car was already in the driveway. They were back from the doctor but they hadn't texted me?

"Do you want to come over?" Becca asked.

"I should probably see how Austin's doing."

"Right, right. I've been thinking about him all week. Is there anything I can do to help? Anything I can bring over? Bubbe just made some chocolate babka this morning."

My stomach rumbled at the sound of that, but I shook my head. If things hadn't gone well today at the doctor's, I was afraid Austin would be too upset for company. Even Becca. "I don't think that would be a good idea."

"Okay." Becca's voice sounded flat.

I turned to head toward my house.

"Wait—Emma?"

I spun around. Becca had her arms folded across her chest. "Text me when you find out, right?"

"Of course."

But Becca was still looking at me funny. If I didn't know her better, I'd say she was about to start crying.

"Becca, what is it?"

"It's just . . . you didn't want me at the hospital. And you didn't want to come over to my house. Ever since you started hanging out with them, I just . . ."

Them? Who did she mean? My family? "What are you talking about?"

"Nothing," she said. But obviously it wasn't nothing because her face was getting red and her voice had gone up an octave.

"Becca, I had to stay with Austin in the hospital. He's my brother, and he was hurt. You didn't miss much, promise. Besides, hospitals are gross. I mainly just fell asleep on my mom." I glanced back toward my house, somehow both eager and nervous to find out what had happened at the doctor's.

"You should just go. Sorry. I'm—I shouldn't have even said anything. I always get like this before my—" She didn't finish the sentence, but I knew what word she'd left off.

Except she'd never said anything before. We had promised we'd tell each other when we got our first period. Why hadn't she told me?

"Never mind, okay?" Becca said. "Just pretend I never said any of this."

"Okay . . . ," I said, finally heading up the walkway to my house.

"Austin, calm down," Mom said. Even from in the entryway, I could hear them like they were right in front of me.

"No!"

I crept into the kitchen, out of sight of the two of them in the living room, and filled up a water glass at the fridge.

Mom was clearly trying her best to be calm, but Austin was testing her. "We have to look at the positives. Remember what the surgeon said? You'll be back in time for the end of basketball season, A. And you'll have the full track season to rebuild and strengthen and—"

"I don't care about track. That's *your* thing. Stop pushing it on me, all right?"

"Austin . . ."

Austin slouched on the sofa, his right arm in a sling. His eyes were puffy from crying, even though Austin never cried. Not even when Grandpa Bill died and he spoke at his funeral.

"When's the surgery?"

I meant to ask Austin, but it was Mom who answered, "Not until just after Christmas."

"Merry Christmas to me, huh?" Austin sighed.

I stared at my brother, trying to come up with the right thing to say. But there wasn't anything to say that would make him feel better. It sucked, plain and simple. If someone took art away from me, I'd throw a full-on tantrum too.

"That sucks," I said.

Mom eyeballed me. "Emma. Language."

"Oh, come on. She said 'sucks,' all right? It's not like we never hear you or Dad swear."

I sat next to him on the sofa. "Will you get to miss school?"

Austin glanced up at Mom.

"The recovery from surgery should allow you to be back in school after New Year's. But how about this: you can have tomorrow off. Let's call it a mental health day."

"Can I have one too?" I asked.

"Do you have a torn labrum?" Mom asked.

"No," I said meekly.

"As it is, this temporary disability is going to throw

a wrench in your studies, A. I know Savannah means well, but I don't want to take advantage of her. You know, I'll call the front office tomorrow and see if there's anyone else who can help."

"Great. So some rando can shadow me all day and take notes for me?"

"Can I help?" I said. "With homework and stuff?"

"I'll learn to write with my left hand before I'm letting a sixth grader do my assignments for me. No offense, Em."

The thought of asking if Becca could help flitted across my mind. Though if Austin didn't want my help, he probably wouldn't want Becca's either.

Mom made sure Austin was okay and told us she needed to run over to the store for a few hours. Once she'd left, Austin turned on the TV, flipping through the channels for a while before settling on a *Saturday Night Live* rerun.

I should've gotten started on my homework, but instead I stayed on the couch with Austin. The episode was a good one, too, with Melissa McCarthy. With each skit, Austin calmed down more. First laughing just a little, then laughing so hard he grimaced because the laughter shook his shoulder.

I was nervous about his surgery—none of us had needed surgery before, not even Mom or Dad—but relieved he didn't seem annoyed at me anymore.

We watched Austin's and my favorite skit twice, the one where Melissa dresses up as Barb Kellner and tries to start a business for eating old pizzas. BARB KELLNER, PIZZA EATER, it would say on the side of her van. It reminded me of Kennedy and her obsession with our middle school's cafeteria rolls, so I searched for it on YouTube and texted it to her.

Life goals, she wrote back.

It was only the next morning as I headed out the door that I realized I'd forgotten to text Becca about Austin.

CHAPTER SIX

A complete labrum tear. That's what the specialists said. Basically, Austin's tendon wasn't attached to the bone anymore and the only way they could reattach it was with surgery. They needed to wait a few weeks for the inflammation to calm down, plus there were the holidays, so the earliest they could get him in was December 27.

But the truth is, as nervous as I was about the surgery, it went fine. The weird part was how Austin acted when they brought him home from the hospital. He was like one of those zombies from *The Walking Dead*—not that I've actually seen the show. Too scary. Still, the zombie version of Austin talked all funny, slurring his words. And even weirder were his delayed reactions. How it took him longer to laugh at something funny. And how he couldn't follow a conversation—he was always two steps behind.

Dad said it was because he was on some strong painkillers and that he'd be like that for only a few days, which was true, but still, it freaked me out. It was unsettling, seeing someone you know well act so out of character.

But by the time we returned to school after break, Austin mostly seemed like his old self. Sure, he couldn't play with the basketball team, but he was still going to practice and games to cheer on his teammates. And Savannah was over all the time, helping him with assignments.

Maybe, if I could go back and find the first sign that something had changed, it was that first Tuesday in February. I don't know what it is about February, but even though it has the fewest days of any month, somehow it always feels the longest.

Every day was cold and gray. Icy snow that refused to melt crusted the edges of the sidewalks in town. The sun was setting well before five, so by the time art club was over, it was too dark to walk back home alone. Dad had been covering for Shannon Malone, the early-morning meteorologist who was out on maternity leave, so he was home in the afternoon to pick me up from school.

That Tuesday as I hopped into his Audi, he asked if I wanted to go out for ice cream. "Do you have bad news or something?" I asked.

Dad chuckled.

"I'm serious. We're not a random 'going out for ice cream after school' kind of family."

Dad pouted. "Didn't realize I needed a reason to grab a milkshake with my favorite girl. My mistake. Should we just head home, then?" he asked with a smile.

"No." I laughed. "Now I'm hungry for a milkshake."

"That's my girl."

After savoring our milkshakes—coffee for Dad, vanilla for me—we grabbed a chocolate one for Austin.

When we got home, Savannah's car wasn't parked in front of our house as usual, so I offered to bring up Austin's milkshake. I wanted to tell him about the band showcase Kennedy invited me to, which was happening at her old school over February break, and how Lucy had a crush on one of the boys in this band called Strawberry Jammin'. Kennedy thought it was the dorkiest band name ever, but I thought it was kind of cute. I liked to picture a little strawberry behind a drum kit, and another with a bass guitar.

The only concert I'd ever been to was at Fenway Park. Mom had tickets to see Pearl Jam with Betsy from the store, but at the last minute Betsy couldn't make it, so she took me. I couldn't understand *any-thing* the singer guy was saying, but I guess Mom did.

The door to Austin's room was closed. I stopped right outside, straining to hear if he was watching a movie on his iPad, which he'd been doing a lot lately. Had he fallen asleep?

"Austin?"

I heard a mumble from inside, so I pushed the door open a crack. It was weird, opening the door to Austin's room, but it was still hard for him to get up and do it himself.

He was propped up in bed with his iPad on his lap, his cell phone next to him. The upper-left corner of the Modest Mouse poster had fallen down. It was the kind of thing Austin would've usually reached up and fixed right away—he loved that poster—but that would require two healthy arms. Scattered across his bed were schoolbooks and magazines—*Rolling Stone* and *Sports Illustrated*—plus two empty Pop-Tarts sleeves and a bag of tortilla chips.

"What?" he snapped. His eyes had dark circles under them and they looked runny.

"Are you okay?"

"Am I *okay*? Hmm, Emma. I can't move my arm. I'm missing most of basketball season. We just dropped a game to Concord-Carlisle, which you know would never happen if I was playing, oh, and because things weren't already crappy enough, Savannah just dumped me."

I gasped. "She did?"

"Guess nobody gives a crap when I'm not the quarterback or the—"

"That's not true, A. She's a jerk. She's a big—"

"Just stop, all right? You don't know anything, Emma." He reached with his left arm for the water bottle on his nightstand, but it toppled over, landing on the floor with a thunk before rolling out of reach.

"Dammit." He closed his eyes, slamming the back of his head against the headboard.

"Austin."

"I can't do anything for myself. Do you know how that feels?"

Now it was my eyes that were smarting as I grabbed the water bottle and held it out to him. Austin snatched it from my hand. His good arm was still plenty strong.

"Just go, Emma. I don't . . . I just can't. Not right now."

So I did.

It wasn't until I was back in my room that I realized I was still holding the milkshake we'd brought back for him.

I sat on the edge of my bed, sucking down that chocolate milkshake and thinking about all the things I did for Austin. All those basketball and football games. Those cold nights in the stands. The blowout games we could've left in the third quarter.

What did I get in return? No, really?

I didn't tear his labrum. I didn't break up with him. How come I was the one he was yelling at, then? Just because I was there? That wasn't fair.

I sucked harder, slurping up the last of the milkshake, until all that was left was air.

You don't know anything, Emma.

I aimed the empty cup for my trash can and watched as it rattled in there. A three-point shot. Better than Austin could do right now.

CHAPTER SEVEN

Any other time, Austin would've been the one to drive me to the band showcase at Kennedy and Lucy's former school the Friday night leading into February break. But with his shoulder not fully healed, he still couldn't drive. And maybe, if I'm going to be totally honest, there were other reasons too.

Since the day Savannah broke up with him, when he blew up at me, I'd been avoiding him. Not entirely, of course. Most nights he still ate dinner with us. But after? When we'd both be upstairs in our rooms doing homework? He'd started closing the door to his bedroom more. Something he used to do only when Savannah was over.

Now that I was in the gym at Comey Valley Charter, watching Strawberry Jammin' for myself,

I could see why Kennedy didn't think that was the right name for them. Strawberries made me think of summer, but there was nothing summery about their music. It was kind of dark. Moody, even.

Kennedy had dyed that one chunk of her hair an electric blue and woven in a few feathers. She was bopping her head to the beat.

"That's him," Lucy whispered in my ear. "Leo. The singer."

His hair was curly, just long enough to tuck behind his ears, and he was wearing thick black plastic glasses. He leaned into the mic, shouting lyrics to some song I didn't know yet but somehow already liked, and strumming on his electric guitar.

Behind the drums sat a boy wearing a black beanie and the kind of vintage band shirt my dad would sometimes wear on weekends. Though I couldn't make out what band. I couldn't stop watching him. The way his tongue would creep out the corner of his mouth the tiniest bit. Like he was concentrating so, so hard at keeping the rhythm even. The drummer holds everything together, doesn't he? Like the glue of the band?

I think Austin said that before.

If I were making a shadow box for Strawberry Jammin', what would go in it? After I told them to get a new name, I mean. I think the background could be a vintage T-shirt. Something threadbare from Goodwill. I could put some guitar picks inside it. Maybe a drumstick or two. And then maybe, maybe if I had the lyrics to their songs, I could cut them out, glue a few of them to the inside of the glass.

Yeah, that could work.

When their set ended, CVC's music teacher stepped up to the mic. "Coming up next, in about fifteen minutes, the Lavenders!" Off in the shadows, a girl with a purple T-shirt knotted above her high-waisted jeans had an acoustic guitar slung over her back. She was talking to a few other girls, also wearing various shades of purple, including one who was twirling drumsticks. An all-girl band? We needed to stick around for them.

"Want to go grab a drink?" Kennedy asked.

I peeked back at the drummer as he got up from the drum set. He picked off his beanie, holding it in his teeth, and ran his fingers through his perfect, thick brown hair.

"Earth to Emma?"

"Sorry," I said.

"No you're not." Kennedy laughed. "You have a crush."

"What?" Even though it was kind of cold in the gym, I could feel my face flush. "No, I don't."

"Wow, you are a horrible liar. Like, really. Don't ever try to work for the CIA, Emma."

"On Noah?" Lucy asked. "Noah Sullivan? *Little* Noah Sullivan?" She played with the tiny orange woolen paws dangling from her fox hat.

"He's not so little anymore," Kennedy said. "A lot can happen in five months, huh? He looks more like his older brother."

I couldn't stop my eyes from darting back in his direction. He was dismantling his drum kit so the next band could set up. What was wrong with me? No, like, really. This had never happened with any boy back at my school. They were all so . . . I don't know, familiar. And none of them had had growth spurts yet. They still looked like fifth graders.

"Let's go get that drink," I said. "I'm thirsty."

"Yeah," Kennedy said. "Thirsty for Noah Sullivan."

"Ew. Stop." I smacked her as we headed into the hallway.

Students were selling water, soda, and baked goods to raise money for a local animal shelter. We bought waters and an enormous M&M chocolate chip cookie to split between the three of us and found a quiet spot to sit against some lockers.

"You should go say hi to him, Emma." Kennedy broke the cookie into thirds. Well, sort of thirds. More like a half and two quarters. Lucy lunged for the largest piece.

"Say hi to him? No way." I took a bite of cookie.

"What's the worst that could happen?" Kennedy asked.

Spontaneous combustion.

"I don't know . . . ," I said. "What would I even say next? After hi, I mean?"

Kennedy ran her tongue over her teeth to get at a piece of red M&M. "You could say that you liked his band. You could ask how long he's played the drums. You could ask . . . anything, Em. He's just a person."

"A cute boy person," I said. "That's the difference."

"What, and Austin's never had any cute friends?" Kennedy asked.

"Ken's right," Lucy said. "You've one hundred percent definitely talked to a cute boy before. It would be humanly impossible not to unless you never left your house. And you do leave your house."

"Em," Kennedy said, nodding. "Em!"

"What?" Did I have chocolate stuck to my teeth too?

"He's about to walk by us," Kennedy said.

"Who?" I asked.

Kennedy rolled her eyes. "The Pope."

The Pope?

"Noah, Em. Noah!" she whisper-yelled.

I jerked my head around and there he was. Along with the bassist from Strawberry Jammin'. The two of them were carrying the kick drum, Noah leading the way.

"Be brave, Emma," Kennedy said, before shoving the last bite of cookie in her mouth.

My heart was in my throat. Or maybe, maybe that was just some cookie. I should've had more water. But if I took a sip now, I'd miss my chance. "Hey," I said, surprised by the sound of my own voice. Was it always that high? "You guys were really good."

His head pivoted toward me. He had the most

beautiful hazel eyes, like something out of a painting in a museum. "Thanks," he said, and then he did this funny thing with his mouth, halfway between a grimace and a smile. "I kinda botched that last song."

"I couldn't even tell."

"That makes me feel better."

"Let's move it, Sully. However strong you think I am, I'm not," his bandmate said.

"Got to go," Noah said to me, and then they continued down the hall.

Kennedy grabbed my shoulders the second they were out of earshot. "I knew you could do it."

"I didn't barf or explode!"

"Were those things maybe going to happen?" Lucy laughed.

"I don't know," I said. "I don't talk to cute boys. I told you!"

"Well, that is certifiably false." Kennedy wiped some crumbs off her shirt. "Because you just did."

"Hey, I think the Lavenders are starting up." Just as Lucy said it, I heard a guitar softly strumming. "Time to head back in?"

The Lavenders weren't the kind of band you stood

around for. Everyone was sitting in groups on the floor, and so we sat down, the three of us, twenty feet or so back from the stage. I stretched my legs out in front of me, knocking my feet together to the beat. Lucy was playing with the strings from her hat. Kennedy had taken out a Sharpie and was drawing little stars all over the back of her right hand.

Suddenly, I could picture it. Like a fast-forward of my life. Me and Kennedy and Lucy. I could see us together in high school, going to a party. I couldn't imagine drinking or most of the other stuff that happens at those parties Austin goes to, but I could imagine us. Our trio. My . . . my herd.

The next morning, I stopped by Becca's for my usual second breakfast. Becca's Bubbe probably wondered why on earth my parents never seemed to feed me breakfast on Saturdays. Well, if she did, she never said anything. Anyway, it was pretty much her fault for making the most delicious challah French toast on the planet. Who could say no to that? Not my stomach.

Becca and her family were leaving for Paris later

that afternoon for all of February vacation. It wasn't like I actually wanted to swap families with Becca, but every time they went on fancy vacations, I couldn't help but be a little jealous.

We O'Malleys hardly went anywhere. Mom never trusted leaving the store for too long, and even though he had to travel to cover big storms, my dad didn't really like flying. We went down to the Cape every summer for a week or two, but that was about it.

"I wish I could go to Paris," I said, sitting cross-legged on Becca's bed.

Her suitcase was still open on the trunk by the window. Sweaters, shirts, and jeans neatly rolled, all ready for the trip.

She sat down on the other side, one leg tucked beneath her, the other dangling free. "I'm actually kind of nervous this time."

"Nervous? Why?"

"You know . . . after last summer . . ."

There had been a terrorist attack in the summer, but it wasn't in Paris; it was on the other side of France. "I'm sure you'll be fine," I said. "It's Paris! The Eiffel Tower, the Louvre. It'll be amazing. Oh!" I said, suddenly thinking of something else amazing. “I have to tell you about last night.”

“What happened last night?”

“I went to this band showcase over at Ken and Luce’s old school and there was this boy named Noah and . . .” I told her all of it. Or at least, I tried to. It was hard to put it into words, exactly, how it felt like this whole new chapter of my life started last night. I hopped off the bed and reenacted everything.

“But you barely talked to him,” she said. “Do you think you’ll ever see him again?”

“I don’t know,” I said. “Maybe? Maybe not. But that isn’t even the point.”

“What is the point, then?” she asked plainly.

“That something was finally happening. For once, in my life. It felt like anything could happen. You know?”

“He’s just a boy, though. We have those at our school too.”

Ugh, she was being so logical. Too logical. Too Becca.

“Maybe it was one of those things where you just had to be there,” I said.

“Guess so.” The way she said it stung. And for the

first time it occurred to me that maybe it bothered her, me hanging out with Kennedy and Lucy so much on the weekends. Even though Becca and I still walked to school together every day and I still came over for second breakfast every Saturday.

"It was just exciting, you know? I want my life to be more exciting."

Just then something caught my eye in Becca's suitcase. Sticking out of the corner was the familiar pale blue and pink of her kitty blanket. That old thing used to be thick and filled with cotton back when we were little, but now it was thin and worn, soft as an old T-shirt. I knew she still slept with it sometimes in fifth grade, but come on. We were middle schoolers now. "You're bringing this to Paris?"

Becca pulled it out of my hands and stuffed it back into her suitcase, but not before rubbing it between her thumb and forefinger. "So? You're wearing your lucky sweatshirt."

"That's different."

"How is it any different? When they're on a winning streak, baseball players will go days without shaving or changing their socks or lucky underwear."

"Becca, that's totally different. They're . . ."

"They're what?"

Professional athletes, for one. Millionaires. Cooler than you or I will ever be. But I didn't say any of that. "Becca, it's a baby blanket."

"It's not like I'm going around wearing it as a cape or something. Now, *that* would be weird. So what? I pack it in my suitcase and bring it to Paris. It's not hurting anyone. Who even knows?"

"Well, for one, if someone inspects your suitcase, they're totally going to see it."

"And? It's not like we know the people working customs at Logan or Charles de Gaulle."

She had a point. "I guess."

There was a knock on Becca's door, and her mom peeked her head in. Dr. Grossman always dressed like she was heading off to some special occasion: the prettiest blouses, heels, neatly pressed pants. Even though she was going to spend the rest of the day on an airplane, she still looked like she'd stepped out of a catalog. "We need to leave shortly for the airport, Rebecca. Oh, hi, Emma! How's your brother doing? Is his shoulder healing all right?"

"I think," I said. According to Mom, who was the one who drove Austin to all of his physical therapy appointments, his shoulder was healing just fine. It was the rest of Austin I was a little worried about. He'd seemed really bummed out and irritable lately.

Dr. Grossman's cell phone rang. "Sorry, girls, guess vacation doesn't start until I put this thing on airplane mode." She ducked back into the hallway.

"I should probably go," I said to Becca. "Take so many pictures!"

"I will," she said.

"Maybe you'll meet a cute boy there. A cute French boy. Ooh la la!"

"Maybe," Becca said. But she didn't sound nearly as excited as Ken or Luce would've been.

Snow began to lightly fall as I made my way down the street. For the short walk home, I couldn't stop thinking about that blanket. I don't know how it had taken me so long to notice, but that day, it felt like a sign. Proof that Becca wasn't ready to grow up yet. And I was.

CHAPTER EIGHT

Becca's flight got out before the snow worsened, dumping a good foot and a half over most of greater Boston. Snowstorms were pretty much what my dad lived for, but for the rest of us, it meant being stuck inside.

Kennedy and Luce lived on the other side of town, and hardly any of the side roads were plowed out, so it wasn't until Tuesday that we could get together. Dad was at the station and Mom was at the store, but Austin was home.

When Kennedy invited me over, I was downstairs watching TV. Austin still had another month or so till he'd be allowed to drive again.

I knocked on his bedroom door to let him know where I was going. "A?" I asked.

A small thump came from inside his room.

Knocking again, I repeated his name.

"I'm busy," he said. But the words didn't sound right. They sounded slurred. Almost like how he'd sounded when he got back from his surgery. "On the phone."

For someone supposedly on the phone, he didn't seem to be doing much talking.

"I'm going over to Kennedy's. Lucy's stepdad's giving me a ride there and back. Mom and Dad know—I texted them."

He said something back, but I couldn't make it out.

"Bye," I said.

As I headed down the stairs to wait for my ride, I had this gnawing feeling that maybe something was wrong. I couldn't put together why exactly, only for the first time I could remember, I felt uncomfortable being in the house, just Austin and me. Used to be, that was the most fun thing I could imagine. Just me and Austin, no parents around to enforce any rules. Austin could play his music as loud as he wanted. I could eat my favorite Trader Joe's mac and cheese for every meal.

But all I noticed now, as I sat peering out the front window, was the eerie quiet of the house. If there was one thing my brother wasn't, it was quiet.

By the time Lucy's stepdad was pulling into the driveway, though, excitement over hanging out with my new friends replaced that fading uncomfortable feeling.

Kennedy's house was an old Victorian, the kind Mom always rooted for the couples on *House Hunters* to choose. Posters of Ken's two favorite figure skaters, Yuzuru Hanyu and Shoma Uno, hung above her bed, and pasted over her desk were sketches of anime characters: action shots, faces, close-ups of their eyes. An enormous bookcase filled with manga and graphic novels was tucked into a corner. The best part: Kennedy had the entire third floor all to herself.

Well, maybe not *all* to herself.

"Lincoln," Kennedy hissed. "What did I tell you? Get out of here."

Her little sister had sneaked up the stairs for the third time in the past fifteen minutes. "Mom!" Kennedy shouted. "Linc's not leaving us alone." She shot her sister a glare.

Lincoln was five years younger than Kennedy, just a first grader, and it took me less than a second to realize how much she looked up to her big sister. Her face radiated when Kennedy introduced her to me. All she wanted was to hang out with the big kids.

But she was still just a first grader. She wouldn't understand half the jokes in the new season of *Haikyu!!* that Kennedy had just paused. Plus we wanted to be able to talk about middle school stuff.

Was it like that for Austin when I was that young? Did it still feel like that sometimes even now? Was that why he'd seemed so irritated with me lately?

The age gap between us felt huge when I was a little kid, but now that I was in middle school, it felt smaller. Like it was closing, even though it wasn't. We'd always be five years apart. But maybe that was only how it felt to me.

Soft footsteps on the stairs meant Lincoln's time with us was dwindling. Her goofy grin turned into a pout as Mama K emerged from the stairwell.

"I don't want to go!" Lincoln whined.

"Linc, the girls need some time to themselves. You can visit with them later, right?"

Kennedy sighed. “Fine.”

“How about we do something special downstairs, just you and me. Bake some cookies?”

Lincoln’s eyes widened at that word. Mama K flashed us a thumbs-up, and they headed downstairs.

“Finally!” Kennedy collapsed on the full-body pillow and propped herself up with her elbows. “Sorry about that. I love her, I do. Just—Lord, she’s been such a pain lately. I know she’s only seven, but she still sucks her thumb. In public! And my moms let her. I swear, she’ll still be sucking her thumb in sixth grade.”

I grabbed a handful of popcorn. “If no one makes you stop, you’ll just do it forever. Like Becca. She still has her baby blanket.” It came out before I’d even thought twice about it.

Kennedy coughed and grabbed her Sprite, taking a big swig. When she finally got her coughing fit under control, she said, “No!”

“It’s not *that* big a deal,” Lucy said quietly, twisting her hair into two buns. If I ever tried to do that, I’d end up looking like a toddler, but somehow when she did it, it looked cool.

"I'm sorry—yes it is. Her *baby* blanket?" Kennedy shook her head.

I could feel my ears warming as the guilt crept in. But wait a second. What did I have to feel guilty for? I was only making a point, a completely valid point. If no one forces you to give up your weirdo little-kid habits, you *will* keep doing them all the way into middle school. It wasn't *my* fault Becca still had her baby blanket.

"Wait, does she really *still* have it?" Kennedy stared at me.

"I think so?" I said, even though of course I knew so. I'd just seen it myself. But it was the next lie that I couldn't so easily excuse. "I haven't been over to her house lately to look or anything. We don't hang out that much anymore." I couldn't let Ken think I regularly hung out with someone who still had something so babyish.

Kennedy lay back down on her pillow. "I mean . . . it's one thing for Lincoln to suck her thumb. But to still be carrying around your baby blanket when you're in middle school? Sorry, but that's messed up. What's she going to do when she goes to college? Take that thing with her? Get married with it?"

"Actually—" Lucy tried to butt in.

"Oh my gosh, Emma. That's too funny."

"Yeah. It's weird."

"Well, enough about baby blankets and thumb sucking," Kennedy said. "*Haikyu!!* time!" And with that, she pushed play.

For the next six hours, only bathroom breaks and the smell of chocolate chip cookies could distract us from our show.

As we passed by Becca's on the way to my house, my stomach clenched. I hated that I still felt guilty for telling Ken and Luce about the kitty blanket. Especially when Becca was so okay with it in the first place!

"Does your family have any big plans for the rest of break?" Mr. Kovacs asked.

"Not really," I said. "I'll probably help my mom out at the store." As we pulled into my driveway, my mind returned to Austin and that weird feeling I'd had earlier. Both Mom's and Dad's cars were in the driveway now, and the house was all lit up, like normal. It was unfair, really, how outsides and insides could tell such different stories.

“There’s a new Studio Ghibli movie opening on Friday,” Lucy said. “Want to go? I bet my sister could take us. She loves their stuff. Plus, last time, she took me and Ken to the theater in Brookline and it’s next to a place with the best Nutella-banana crepes on the planet.”

My stomach grumbled yes for me. Lucy grinned. “Okay, I’ll text her and Ken.”

“Sounds good,” I said, reaching for the door handle. “Thanks for the ride!” I told Lucy and her stepdad.

Heading toward my house, my breath little dragon puffs in the cold air, I suddenly remembered how Lucy had been trying to say something while Kennedy was going on and on about the baby blanket. It was hard for her to get a word in sometimes. Kennedy could just talk and talk forever.

Part of me wished she’d invited just me to go with her and her sister to the movie. Even though we’d been friends for a few months, I still hadn’t spent time with her without Kennedy. What was she like, just on her own?

Inside, I took off my shoes and jacket. I heard hushed voices upstairs.

"This is junior year, bud. You can't afford to let your grades slip like this. College application season will be here before you know it."

"It was just one test!"

"That's not true, A. Dad and I can see everything on the portal. You're not turning assignments in. And if you're not doing the work, of course it's going to show on exams. In any case, there's still time—"

"I don't care."

"Austin." Mom's tone softened.

"I don't."

"What kind of attitude is that?" Dad raised his voice. "Of course you care. You've always cared. Look, I know this injury has been hard, but these things happen. No one sails through life without a few bumps in the road."

I went into the living room and turned on the TV, shifting the volume high enough so I couldn't hear them.

Mom and Dad were trying not to be too hard on Austin, but it wasn't working. His surgery was almost two months ago. Things were supposed to be getting back to normal by now.

Except they weren't. Not doing his homework? Getting a bad grade on a test? That wasn't Austin. He wasn't some stereotype of a football player who barely knows the alphabet. Dad liked to boast how Austin had the second-highest GPA on the team. Sure, he was no Becca, but really, who was?

But the past few weeks he'd stopped going to basketball games to cheer on his teammates. And even when he was home, he was always in his room with the door closed. What was he doing in there if he wasn't doing homework? Sleeping? *That* much?

Upstairs, a door slammed. Austin turned up his music. I muted the TV, the chocolate chip cookies suddenly heavy in my stomach.

"I don't know what to do anymore, Tony. The more we push, the more he pushes back."

"Maybe this is just a phase. It happens sometimes with boys his age. Let's try backing off a bit. See if that helps."

"I don't know . . ."

"It can't hurt to try."

"Have you heard from Emma? Do we need to pick her up?"

"I think I heard the front door open a minute ago." Dad raised his voice: "Hey, Emma?"

I got up from the couch. "Yeah?"

When Mom came down, her smile looked fake, like her mind was still upstairs with Austin. "Have fun at Kennedy's?"

"Yeah." I suddenly wished I was back at the Novaks', where the biggest tension was over whether or not a seven-year-old was going to unexpectedly bust into the room.

"You have dinner over there?"

I shook my head. "Just a bunch of cookies."

"Ooh, cookies!" Mom's smile turned authentic. "What kind?"

"Chocolate chip."

"Sounds delish. Let's see if we can rustle up something for dinner. Give me a hand?"

"Sure." I flicked off the TV and followed Mom into the kitchen. She stuck her head in the fridge, pulling out vegetables for a salad while I grabbed place mats, plates, and silverware to set the table. "Hey, Mom?"

She stopped chopping bell pepper for a second.

"Is everything okay with Austin?"

Mom's mouth settled somewhere between a smile and a frown. "He's going to be fine. We're just in a rough patch right now. Nothing for you to worry about, okay?"

"But if there was, you know you could tell me, right? I'm in middle school now. I can handle it."

"You're an awful lot more mature than Austin was at your age, that's for sure. Tell me more about Kennedy's—what's her family like? What did you all do?"

That quickly I knew I wasn't going to get more out of Mom about Austin.

CHAPTER NINE

For Christmas, Austin had given me tickets for the Picasso exhibit at the Museum of Fine Arts in late March. Two tickets, though it was a given that I would take him.

Ever since I was old enough to ride the trains with him into Boston without Mom or Dad, it became a thing we did. Take the commuter train to the T into Cambridge or Boston to check out an exhibit at a museum or catch a Red Sox, Bruins, or Celtics game. It wasn't something we did all the time. Austin was busy—well, he used to be busy. It was something special. Like a date. Except not a date, because he was my brother.

But here we were, the final weekend of the Picasso exhibit. And my date—my brother—was standing me up.

"He was supposed to be home by now," I mumbled, staring at all the unanswered texts I'd sent my brother. I was sitting on the couch in the living room, all dressed and ready to go.

Where are you?

We're going to be late.

Austin, come on.

Where. Are. You.

He was supposed to be back two hours ago. That would have given him enough time to shower, shave, and get dressed before we took the commuter rail to the T so we could be at the museum by two p.m.

The trains didn't run that often on Sundays, and even on the weekdays this winter, the T had been a mess.

"If you want, I can come with you." Dad turned down the volume on the March Madness game. "Just say the word and I can—" He stopped to cough, a gross hacking one full of phlegm. He'd spent most of the weekend on the couch while Mom went into the city, getting wined and dined by running-sneaker salespeople swinging through Boston.

"No, he's coming. He promised. Plus, Dad . . . you're sick."

He cleared his throat and smiled. "I can rally with the best of them."

"You'd be that guy on the T everyone's afraid of because you're coughing all over the place. Thanks, though."

He turned the volume back up. The coaches paced the sidelines, like how Austin's coach used to. He probably still did; I just hadn't been to any games this season. UCLA was playing Cincinnati and it was a close game, not that I cared or really knew much about college basketball. Austin and Dad used to watch the games together on the weekends all the time, but not since he'd quit the team.

I touched my phone screen to wake it back up. I don't know why I kept doing that. It would wake up with a message, a quick vibration if Austin texted me back. Or make that awful whistling teakettle sound if someone called. Kennedy had sneakily changed it at lunch the other day and I kept forgetting to change it back.

I checked the PDF of the train schedule again. We'd already missed the train we'd been planning to take, but there was still another that left an hour later.

We wouldn't have a lot of time at the museum, but it wasn't like I needed to see any other exhibits. It was only the sold-out Picasso exhibit that would be leaving soon. The next day, actually.

I swallowed down that tickling feeling in the back of my throat. Told myself it was just Dad's cold coming for me even though it felt like something worse.

My phone buzzed on my lap, sending my heartbeat skipping. Maybe Austin was on his way. Letting me know he'd showered at his friend's house and that we could take an Uber into the city to make up time.

But it was a text from Becca. Want to go to Starbucks? My dad can take us.

I slammed my phone down on the sofa. Ever since she got back from Paris, things had been weird between us. We still walked to school together, but I'd started skipping my second breakfasts at her house on Saturdays. The truth was, I couldn't forget those things Kennedy said about her over February break. Never mind the lie I told Kennedy about how we hadn't hung out in a while.

I couldn't imagine not being friends with Becca,

but I also couldn't imagine how things would be for us if she never changed. Kennedy had a point. Was she going to keep sleeping with that kitty blanket all through high school?

But it was about more than the blanket too. There were other ways Becca was starting to seem immature. Even though she was still probably the smartest person I knew. I wanted to be able to talk about crushes without her getting all weirded out—or seeming bored by it. I wanted her to care about that and all the other stuff that Kennedy and Lucy did: TV shows and bands and artists. All of it.

It hadn't mattered in elementary school, how Becca and I had such different interests, but lately it kept feeling like it did matter. Like it mattered a lot. Like she didn't really understand me anymore.

And I didn't know how to fix it. I didn't know how to make her be the person I wanted her to be.

"Emma." Dad muted the game. "Really, hon, I'm more than happy to take you into the city. We can drive in. You know what, I'll even swing by CVS and get one of those face masks so I won't infect anyone at the MFA."

My eyes smarted. He didn't get it. This was supposed to be something Austin and I did together, without him or Mom. Like we used to. We had only one more year of it too. And then he'd be off to college somewhere far away. That was what he said when people asked where he wanted to go. Far away from us?

Well, now he was. He might have lived in our house with me and Mom and Dad, but he felt far away.

What college even wanted someone who flunked math their junior year, anyway? Did he ever stop to think about that?

"What do you say, E?"

What I wanted to say was, how long are you going to let him get away with this? But before I had a chance, the loud whistle of a teakettle cut through the quiet. I snagged my phone from the other side of the sofa, ready to let him have it. Everything Mom and Dad had decided to swallow down was ready to come out of me. Pour out and all over him, like a pot of boiling-hot tea.

Except the name flashing across the screen wasn't Austin. And it wasn't Becca either. It was Kennedy.

"Don't worry about it," I said to Dad. I shuffled up the stairs, waiting till I was halfway up before I swiped across to answer the call. "Hey, Ken."

She must have heard something in my voice because right away hers came down a few notches. "Is everything okay?"

"Yeah." I sniffled. I closed my bedroom door behind me, sliding down it until I was on the floor, the back of my head thumping lightly against the door. "No."

"Em, what's wrong?"

I hadn't said anything to her or Lucy about how Austin had been lately. They didn't know him that well, and I guess I figured things would get better, that the way he was acting was temporary. But I wasn't so sure anymore. Sometimes people change and it isn't for the better and they don't go back to the way they were before.

So I told her. How Austin still hadn't come home from the night before with his friends. How my dad was so chill about it. Maybe Mom would've been different if she'd been home, but she was out. My brother hadn't let me down before. Not like this.

I should have seen it coming, with the way he'd been about, well, everything since he got hurt. As if he was the only person who mattered.

"What if I go with you?" Kennedy offered. "Maybe Mama K can take us? She loves the MFA. Let me check."

Her response was the one thing that made me feel less bad about everything. But it wasn't enough. "It's too late," I said. "They close at five."

"I'm sorry, Em. He sucks. Do you want to come over? The moms are getting a pizza. They're about to call it in. We can put pineapple on it for you."

"That's okay. I'm not really hungry."

"Sorry—I gotta go. See you tomorrow?"

"Later."

I peeked at my messages again, even though I knew there weren't any from him. The one from Becca was still there though. Sorry, I wrote back. I'm busy.

I dug through my desk drawer until I found a yellow pad of Post-its. With a fat black Sharpie, I scrawled, *You owe me*, and slapped it on my brother's door.

At four forty-five I heard a loud squeal from a car outside. A moment later the sound of the front door opening and shutting. Dad and Austin exchanged a few words, but what exactly they said, I didn't know. I'd listened in on enough of their conversations lately and it wasn't getting me anywhere.

Heavy footsteps on the stairs—just quick enough to not have been Dad's.

Austin cursed. "That was *today*." A knock on my door. "Emma?"

I hated that I couldn't help myself, hated that tears were streaming down my cheeks like some little kid whose mom had denied them the toy they wanted at Target. I was never that kid who made a scene—not even when I was little. Keeping everything inside was never hard for me. Even when I was a baby, Mom said I was always happy as a clam.

"Emma, come on."

I couldn't let him see me like this. He wouldn't open my door without me saying it was okay. We had rules, me and Austin. A closed door meant you didn't bother the other person.

He stayed there for a while, pacing in the hall right in front of our rooms. Then his phone buzzed and he laughed. *Laughed.*

He sucks.

Right when Kennedy had said it, I'd felt this little pinch. Like, who was she to say my brother sucked? But to laugh? Right now? After what he did?

Kennedy was right.

Austin did suck.

The only person he cared about was himself.

CHAPTER TEN

At lunch on Monday, Kennedy didn't bring up what happened the day before with Austin, and that was fine by me. When I was at school, I didn't want to worry about the person my brother was turning into. (Had turned into?)

While Kennedy picked out the fluffy insides of today's cafeteria rolls, Lucy quietly reached into her backpack and set some kind of catalog in the middle of the cafeteria table. "My stepdad showed me this last night," she said. "What do you think?"

Kennedy snatched it off the table before I even got a good look at it. "Yes. A million times yes."

"What is it?" I asked.

She flashed the cover, which said *RISD Young Artists* in bold, bright colors.

"What's R.I.S.D.?" I asked.

"Riz-Dee," she said. "Rhode Island School of Design. You know, in Providence. Summer. Art. Camp! On the campus and also on the beach. The beach!" Kennedy swooned backward. "Okay, we're going. We're so going. Aggghhh!" She shoveled all the pieces of roll into her mouth so fast I thought she might choke on them.

Right then Haven Mulligan passed by our table. She was one of those girls who was popular even though nobody seemed to actually like her that much. "Spaz much?" She raised her eyebrows at Kennedy. Kennedy raised an eyebrow right back at her. Lucy's cheeks went pink.

By the time Kennedy finished chewing all that roll, Haven had sat down a few tables over with her friends.

I loved how Kennedy didn't even seem to care about them. It was like she was above all that.

"Okay, so, I'll ask the moms tonight," she said. "Em, you in?"

I nodded. Each week at camp meant one fewer week hanging out at the store with Mom. Not that I didn't like hanging out with my mom all summer. It was just that she thought it was super exciting for me to "learn the ropes" because someday the store could be mine if I wanted. But spending part of the summer near the ocean with my friends and real live artists? That beat getting to browse shoe catalogs and double-check inventory, easy.

All day, I couldn't stop imagining what it would be like to learn from someone like Joseph Cornell, except, you know, still alive. Having a whole week—or more if Mom and Dad let me do a couple of the programs—to think, live, and breathe art. And also eat pizza. According to Lucy, whose grandma lived there, Providence had *the best* pizza.

Lucy's grandma taught physics at Brown and had a guest room we could share. The whole thing sounded so perfect I could barely believe it.

Dad was still off work with that gnarly cold, so he swung by school to pick me up, and on the ride home I told him all about it.

"Sounds perfect for you."

"So I can go? For real?"

"Mom and I'll talk it over tonight. And I'd like to chat a bit with Lucy's grandmother, make sure she's really up for having all three of you goons. But assuming she's game, yeah, why not? Speaking of goons, what's Becca got lined up for the summer?"

"Probably going to that camp at Harvard," I replied, staring out the window. I hadn't asked her about it, actually. But given that nothing else about Becca seemed to be changing this year, why would that?

"I know your mom might feel differently, but I get it, E. I remember drifting apart from some of my friends at your age. Remember how close Austin was with Ryan Abreu before he transferred to BB&N? I'm sure if you ever wanted to talk about it with him—"

"Because he's so accessible . . ."

"Emma."

"You didn't even give him a hard time for what happened yesterday."

"That's not true. Mom and I had a good long chat with your brother last night. He's grounded for the next month."

A whole month? I turned back to Dad. He wasn't serious, was he? His mouth formed a firm line as he stared out at the sea of red taillights in front of us.

He cleared his throat. "This winter hasn't been

easy for any of us. But spring's right around the corner, and I'm hoping a change in the weather will make a difference for Austin. Everyone faces adversity at some point in their life, but it's what you do with it that shows your true character."

Since when had my dad turned into a motivational speaker? I pulled out my phone to text Kennedy and Lucy. Dad said yes. He wants to talk with Lucy's grandma. ART CAMP, HERE WE COME! I followed it up with every art-related emoji I could find.

Later that week, on Wednesday, I was all caught up on my homework, snuggled under my comforter with the iPad to watch this scary Netflix show Lucy had told me about, when I heard Austin's door open.

After dinner Mom had run over to the store to help Betsy process a huge shipment of sneakers that had come in ahead of the Boston Marathon, and Dad was playing basketball in his pickup league.

I thought maybe Austin was coming over to hear more about art camp, since Mom registered me today, but as he walked past my room, it sounded like he had sneakers on. What did he think he was doing, sneaking out? He was grounded. Super grounded.

"Austin?"

He stuck his head in my room. "Yeah?"

"You going somewhere?"

"Just heading out for a sec."

Did he think I was born yesterday? "Aren't you grounded?"

He cocked his head, eyeballing me. "What? You on my case now too?"

It was only then that I noticed the dark circles under his eyes. How his skin didn't look as pink and healthy as it used to, but like he was coming down with something.

"No," I said quietly.

I wanted to say something more. Mom and Dad weren't around. It was just us. I should have asked him what was really going on.

"At least someone's still on my team." He wasn't wrong, exactly. I was always on his team. But I hated the way he said it: like Mom and Dad weren't when of course they were.

"Don't say anything to Mom and Dad, okay? I'll be back in ten minutes, tops. And then I'll work on my damn history project, all right?" He thumped his palm on my door before disappearing down the hallway.

I heard the front door open and slam shut, and then the engine of Austin's car—well, Mom's old car—motor up.

I unpaused my show, but I couldn't focus on it. That bad feeling I'd had about my brother on and off ever since February was back, stronger than ever. Except this time he wasn't in his bedroom all by himself with the door closed, saying he was busy when he clearly wasn't.

But maybe this was worse. He was leaving, and I didn't know where he was going. He hadn't even bothered to come up with a lie. No, worse: I hadn't even asked him.

I just let him go.

Was it because I'd gotten used to it? This new version of my brother that had evolved over the past few months? If I stopped and thought about it too much, the truth was, I didn't recognize him anymore. My brother, the one who was always busy before. Who always had a girlfriend. Who always had sports and so many friends but who now spent way too much time in his room, holed up by himself doing who knows what.

I paused my show again to check the time. Only five minutes had passed. I pressed play and watched a scene. Checked again. Ten minutes.

Come on, Austin.

Mom and Dad wouldn't be out all night. They both said they'd be back before I went to bed.

Another ten minutes passed, and I was about to text Austin when I heard a car pull into the driveway. *That better not be Mom or Dad, or you're in for it, A.*

But when the door opened, I heard only one set of footsteps and no "hello." A minute later Austin passed by my room. He didn't pop his head in to say thank you or anything, just went right into his room, closed the door, and turned his music up until I reached for my headphones to plug into the iPad.

You're welcome.

Part of me wanted to go in there and just say that to his face. Spit it right out at him. But then part of me was chicken. Part of me would always want my big brother to love me.

There were a million parts of me that night. But all of them stayed in the bed, deep under the comforter with the iPad. The truth was: I had no idea what happened in the show. All I could think about was Austin.

CHAPTER ELEVEN

Maybe it was knowing I'd spend part of July at the RISD art camp or maybe it was needing something to distract me from whatever was going on with my brother, but that spring I made three new shadow boxes.

One was for Lucy, whose birthday was in April. I wanted something that pulled together all her talents and interests: collage and singing and animals. When I was little, I'd loved Calico Critters, and I still had some deep in my closet. The teeny outfits they came with made them look for sure like little-kid toys, but with some fabric and a glue gun and, okay, Mom's credit card for a few things I found cheap on Etsy, I turned them into a country trio. For the background, I sliced up sample wallpapers my mom had gotten back when she redid the downstairs bathroom. It was a little bit country, a little bit girlie, and somehow, exactly right for Lucy.

Another was for my grandparents out in California. They were in assisted living, close by Mom's sister Kelly, and we didn't see them a ton. My grandma loved to cook, though, so I used her favorite recipe—for buttermilk blueberry muffins—as the backdrop. I'd found a miniature colander and a bunch of blue marbles at a yard sale. The hard part was making sure the marbles didn't roll around. So much glue!

I still didn't know who the last one was for, but I'd found a bird's nest on the ground out back one weekend when I was helping my dad with yard work. He said not to touch it just in case, so I didn't, but once it had sat there for a week, it was fair game.

I wanted this box to be all found objects. Why, I didn't exactly know. Only that it felt right. One afternoon in mid-May on my walk home from school with Becca, I spotted a tiny red mitten. It had probably fallen off some little baby in a stroller in the winter, got buried in the snow, and then been blown all over the place in the spring.

I snatched it up off the ground.

"Ew, Emma. It's probably dirty," Becca said.

"It's not like I'm planning to eat it," I replied, sticking it in my jeans pocket. "It's perfect for my shadow box though. At least, I think."

"Did you turn in your forms for Camp McSweeney yet?" Becca asked.

The annual sixth-grade class trip wasn't for another month yet, but they made us do permission slips early because it involved *a lot* of planning. At least that's what my mom said. She had volunteered for it back when Austin was my age and complained for months. I swear, me just bringing home the permission slip seemed to trigger her.

Right before the last week of the school year, the entire sixth grade would spend three nights on Cape Cod at Camp McSweeney, doing team-building exercises and learning about oceanography. We'd even get to tour a cranberry bog and a potato chip factory. Yeah, they totally had Kennedy at "potato chip." Me too, to be honest.

"Yeah," I said. There was a spot on the form to request a cabin mate. They said it wasn't a guarantee, but if you put your friend's name there, odds were you'd end up bunking in the same cabin.

But they let you put down only *one* name. So we had to strategize. Kennedy put down Lucy. Lucy put down me. And I put down Kennedy.

"Did you?" I asked.

Becca shook her head. "My mom was trying to figure out who to ask about keeping kosher and, well, you know my mom. She got wrapped up in something at work and forgot. Who did you write in?"

"Kennedy," I said. And then probably too quickly: "You hadn't asked and—"

"It's fine," Becca said. "I mean, I can probably still put you down."

"Or you could put down Fern?" She and Fern Robbins had been doing bat mitzvah prep together all spring.

"I guess . . . ," Becca said.

"I just mean your chances are probably better. Especially if you both put each other." I explained our triangle strategy.

"Mathematically true," Becca said, seeing my line of thinking.

The last thing I wanted was for her to think I didn't want her in my cabin, even though a tiny part of me didn't. Especially if it meant I couldn't be with Kennedy and Lucy.

"As long as we're not with Haven Mulligan."

"Right?" I laughed. "I wish there was a way to write that on the form."

"No kidding. Too bad your mom's not volunteering. Hey, so . . . I haven't seen Austin out running in a while. Everything okay with him?"

Ever since I'd told Kennedy about how Austin had let me down, I wished I hadn't. In a way, it was like saying it out loud to someone had made the whole situation real. And that was the last thing I wanted. I wanted him to go back to the way he was before, the brother he'd always been to me.

Becca only knew that Austin. I didn't want her to know this one.

"He's not doing spring track this year," I said, as if that's all that was different.

"Your mom must be so bummed."

"Yeah," I said. "Now the only track star in the family is me." I grimaced.

"Hey, you're better than me. How fast is your mile now?"

"Just under nine minutes." I left off the fact that I was one of the last finishers at every meet.

"That's amazing! Remember in gym class? I could barely finish it in twelve."

"On the plus side, I haven't accidentally stabbed anyone with a javelin . . . yet."

"Good job, Emma. Good job." Becca laughed.

By that point we were at the edge of her driveway. The magnolia tree in front of her house was in full bloom. If there were a way to snap one of those blossoms off and keep it just like that forever, I would 100 percent put it in a box. But there's something sad about dried flowers. At least to me. They only reminded me of the real thing.

"Yikes—I'd better get my homework done. My mom's taking me to Porter Square Books tonight for an author event." Her eyes lit up when she said it.

"Oh, cool. Well, have fun." There was this little pang in my chest. Like part of me wanted to be invited even though I probably didn't know the author, even though I probably hadn't read any of their books. Was that how she felt when I made plans with Kennedy and Lucy?

"See you tomorrow," she said.

As I turned back to head home, I noticed a blossom that had fallen off the tree. Pink and white. Not trampled by anyone. Not yet.

I picked it up and carried it all the way home. Maybe it wasn't going to last, but it was too beautiful to just leave there.

CHAPTER TWELVE

The day before the sixth-grade trip, the door to my brother's room was ajar, for once, when I got home from track. "Hey, A? You have a sec?"

The shades were drawn. When I stepped into his room, my foot crunched a half-eaten bag of . . . I didn't even want to know what. The whole room had a sad smell to it, like wilted french fries and dirty laundry. I guessed that without a girlfriend stopping by, he had nobody to impress. But still.

His laptop sat on the edge of his bed playing a movie, but when I got closer, I could see that Austin's eyes were closed. What was he doing asleep at four in the afternoon? I nudged his shoulder and his eyes fluttered open.

"Geez, you try knocking?" His words came out slowly.

"Your door was open," I said. "And I did." I hated that the second part came out as a whisper. It didn't used to be like this—never knowing when Austin might snap at me.

He rubbed his eyes and reached over to pause his movie. "Guess I nodded off."

I pulled up a shade, thinking some sunlight might wake him up, never mind help with this whole man-cave situation, but all it did was shine a spotlight on what a dump this place had become. I knew Mom and Dad tried to stay out of our rooms, but there could have been a raccoon living in here and you wouldn't even notice.

"So, I leave for Camp McSweeney tomorrow." I sat on the edge of his bed, pulling my knees up to my chest.

"You do know what they say about Camp McSweeney. . . ."

"What do they say?"

"What happens at Camp McSweeney stays at

Camp McSweeney." Austin gave me a serious nod.

"Really? No." I couldn't help scrunching my nose. "Ew. Gross."

"Lot of first kisses happen at Camp McSweeney. Just saying." For a second it felt like we were back in the fall. Like his injury had never happened. But then I blinked and took in our surroundings and knew it was almost summer. That in a week we'd be out of school.

Buh-bye, sixth grade. Hello, seventh. I wondered if Austin felt that way. If he was ready to put eleventh grade behind him, eager for a fresh start.

I grabbed a stray pillow from the end of the bed and chucked it at him. "Stop it."

Austin cracked a smile.

There was no boy in my grade that I wanted to kiss at the moment, that was for sure. None could even come close to Noah Sullivan. I hadn't seen him since the band showcase, but in my head, I was pretty sure I would always see him. Especially those eyes.

Though maybe there'd be someone at camp this summer. A cute artist boy in Rhode Island. Maybe?

"Was your first kiss at Camp McSweeney?"

"I'm not telling you about my first kiss, Em. That stuff is sacred."

"Sacred, huh? Sure. Was it before? After?"

Austin kept shaking his head.

"Oh, come on!"

"You already know who my first kiss was."

"Wait, Savannah?"

He shook his head.

Who was that girl he dated for a few months sophomore year? Her name started with an *H.* Hailey? Heather? Oh wait! "Hannah?"

"Nope, nope, nope. I'll give you a hint. She was your first kiss too."

"That doesn't even make sense. . . ."

"Mom."

I stuck out my tongue. "Ew, and you *know* that's not what I mean."

"Oh, Emma. Don't ever change, okay?" He leaned back in his bed and gave me this funny look, as if beneath his wisecracks was something like wisdom. As if he knew something I didn't yet.

"Yeah," I said as I slipped off his bed. "Well, I better go pack. Enjoy your movie."

On my way out of his room, I walked right by his desk. A test with a *67* circled in red ink stuck out of one of his books. A knot tightened in my stomach. I couldn't unsee it.

The following afternoon, as seventh and eighth graders were filing out of the middle school for their regularly scheduled weekend activities, we sixth graders piled onto school buses in the rear parking lot, our backpacks and duffels stuffed with everything we'd need to survive three days away from home.

Lucy, Kennedy, and I squeezed ourselves into the same bus seat—it helped that Lucy was so tiny. Becca was somewhere up front with Fern.

"I'm so excited!" Kennedy squeezed my shoulders.

"Really? I couldn't tell," Lucy said, anxiously tapping her knees.

One of the science teachers, Mrs. Ryan, stood at the front of the bus and blew a whistle. Quickly, everyone quieted down. "All right, I've got your cabin assignments here." She tapped her iPad. "Please listen carefully so you'll know your chaperone and cabin mates. Now, this is not a perfect science, and I'm sure some of you will be disappointed. But let's remember: this is only for the next three days—not the rest of your lives. Okay?"

"Okay," we chorused.

"Cabin number one, you'll be with Coach Lipinski. Owen Peterson, Jose Sanchez, Ivan Hanigan . . ."

As she read through the lists, Kennedy, Lucy, and I squeezed each other's hands.

"Kennedy Novak." My ears perked up. "Grace Collins. Tilly Weathers. Olivia Vroman. Lucy Chan. Haven Mulligan. Emma O'Malley." *Yes! Yes, yes!* "Becca Grossman."

My heart sank. Had she put my name down? Even after our chat? I thought we agreed it made the most sense for her to put down Fern. But I was 99 percent sure Mrs. Ryan didn't say Fern was in our cabin.

"We made it!" Kennedy danced in her seat. Lucy looked relieved too.

But me? I was craning my neck, trying to see up to the front of the bus. And then suddenly Becca's head popped up. She grinned at me, and somehow I smiled back, but for the whole ride to Cape Cod I could barely focus.

What if she did something to embarrass me? In front of Kennedy and Lucy or, worse, in front of Haven Mulligan.

By the time we arrived at Camp McSweeney, my stomach was growling. Dinner still wasn't for another half hour, so the chaperones led us to our cabins to get settled.

"I call top bunk!" Kennedy yelled.

Our chaperone, Grace Collins's mom, chimed in. "Actually, Kennedy—"

Kennedy flung open the cabin door and frowned. It turned out there weren't bunks at all—more like army cots arranged in rows. And it smelled in there. Like some animal had died over the winter.

Mrs. Collins cracked a few windows to air the place out while we claimed our cots. Becca must've stopped to use the bathroom or something, because by the time she got to the cabin, there was only one cot left, in the back corner across from where Mrs. Collins would sleep.

"It all happened so fast," I said to Becca. It was a stupid excuse, but what I hated was that I even felt guilty in the first place.

But she just shrugged. “I don’t mind,” she said, and it seemed like she really meant it. “The cabins are just for sleeping, anyway.”

Behind her, Grace Collins giggled. “Clearly, *someone*’s never been to a sleepaway camp before.”

She and Haven whispered back and forth, occasionally eyeing Becca, and I thought about what Austin said. What everyone else in our grade knew. But maybe not? Maybe Becca hadn’t picked up on it at all. That Camp McSweeney was totally about us sixth graders trying to pretend we were older. Sneaking out, getting into trouble, first kisses.

And just thinking that made me sad. Sad for Becca, and maybe even a little sad for me. Because now that we were in the same cabin, I knew I’d have to look out for her.

Later that night Mrs. Collins was called away with an “emergency” not long after we’d changed into our pajamas and gotten into our sleeping bags for lights-out. Some kid in another cabin had fallen off a huge rock, and since Mrs. Collins was an ER nurse, she was asked to help. She left Grace in charge until she returned, and Grace was taking full advantage of the situation.

Grace piped up over our chatter. "Guys? Guys. I have an idea. We played this game at camp last summer *all* the time and it's so fun. Want to play?"

Over in her cot at the far end, Becca was already deep in a book. She barely looked up. Every other girl in the cabin, however, was game.

"What's it called?" Kennedy asked.

"Never Have I Ever," Grace said before explaining how it worked. We'd go around in a circle, and when it was your turn, you were supposed to say something you'd never done. But then anyone who actually *had* done that thing had to raise her hand. Basically, it was like truth or dare, minus the dare.

"I'll start," Grace said. She sat cross-legged on her sleeping bag. Now that we'd already washed up, I noticed a cluster of tiny pimples on her forehead that she must have usually covered up with makeup. It made me feel better to see a glimpse of the real Grace Collins. To know even she wasn't as perfect as she tried to be in school. "Never have I ever . . . kissed a boy. Yet." Her eyes darted around at all of us. "Oh, come on! I know someone here has." She stared down Haven until she meekly raised her hand.

Across from me, Tilly Weathers's face was going redder by the second, and she raised her hand too. Girls whispered back and forth.

"Okay," Grace said. "So, let's keep going clockwise. That means . . . Olivia, you're up next."

Olivia tapped on her chin.

"This year, Olivia!"

Gosh, Grace Collins was bossy. Glad I didn't have to hang out with her every day.

"Okay, okay. Just give me a sec, all right? Never have I ever . . . left the country?"

Three hands shot up, including Becca's. I guessed not every "Never have I ever" had to be super personal or juicy. That was a relief.

As girls took turns confessing things about themselves they probably wouldn't if not for bossy Grace Collins, I was stuck trying to figure out what to say when my turn came around. The truth was, I didn't have something secretly cool to confess. And sure, I could say something I wished was true, like I'd met Beyoncé. But what I wanted was for the perfect, clever, funniest thing to be zapped down into my brain, and so far that wasn't happening.

"Kennnnnedy." Grace's voice was all singsongy. How long was her mom going to be gone, anyway?

Kennedy's eyes went large, and for a second I thought Grace had caught her off guard. The Kennedy I knew never got nervous. She chewed on the inside of her cheek. "Wait, I got one. Never do I ever . . . still sleep with my baby blanket."

For a moment I couldn't believe it. She couldn't have said that. Kennedy would *never* say that. Not here. Not to someone like Grace Collins. Not with Haven Mulligan in the room.

But as Grace lifted her hand over her mouth to stifle a giggle, I knew it had happened. "Who would do that?" Her mouth opened wider, the light catching her braces. "We're in sixth grade. Come on."

I knew better than to look at Becca, but somehow I couldn't stop myself from glancing down the row of cots. Tears formed in Becca's eyes, magnified by her glasses.

I sucked a deep breath in through my nose. *No one's looking at Becca besides you, Emma. Just stay calm and pretend you don't see. You can chew out Kennedy later.*

Haven reached out a pointer finger. "I think I can guess who does," she said, her voice breaking into laughter as she pointed right at Becca.

All at once, it was like something out of *Mean Girls*. Becca, climbing out of her sleeping bag, trying to flee to the bathroom, be anywhere but in this cabin. Haven shouting, "Oh my gosh, guys. She *brought it*."

Tilly Weathers. "She did! She *did*."

"Let's see," Haven Mulligan said.

I couldn't see who did it, who had shaken out her sleeping bag. Whether it was Haven or Grace. All I saw was Becca's tattered kitty blanket on the dusty cabin floor and the girls pouncing on it. Waving it in the air like they were playing capture the flag. I was the worst kind of bystander, frozen in place on my cot.

"What on earth is going on in here?" Mrs. Collins stared at us, bewildered. "Girls! Please. Calm yourselves."

As the commotion came to a stop, I locked eyes with Kennedy. *I didn't mean to,* she mouthed.

"That's about enough. We have a long day ahead of us tomorrow, and we're well into quiet hour. Now,

I'm going to turn off the lights. Let's hope that tonight was an anomaly or it's going to be a long three days. Okay, ladies?"

"Yes," half the girls murmured.

"Now, back into your sleeping bags."

In the far corner of the room, Becca's cot was empty, her sleeping bag all bunched up on the floor. The tiny remains of her kitty blanket, trampled.

Had she managed to slip out when all of that was going on? She must have, because she wasn't here now. Had she run into Mrs. Collins outside? Had she told on everyone? Or had she only escaped to the bathroom to wait it out?

Mrs. Collins flicked the light switch and then we were in the dark. Cots creaked as girls tried to get comfortable. A few of them still whispered, but Mrs. Collins shushed them sharply and they shut up. I buried my face in my pillow. There was no way I could fall asleep after what had happened. This was going to be the longest night of my life.

I hated myself for ever saying anything to Kennedy and Lucy. And even more, for all the feelings I had about Becca that I couldn't stop. Why had every little thing about Becca started to bother me so much? It never had before.

She was my friend. My oldest friend.

Was.

Was that all in the past now? The Becca-and-Emma days? Maybe it was. And realizing that felt worst of all.

In the dark, as the girls around me drifted off to sleep, I lost all sense of time. But eventually there was a tap at the door and Mrs. Collins stepped outside. Soon after, Becca came in and climbed onto her cot.

One of the girls whispered in the softest voice, "Meow." Another giggled.

"Hey!" Mrs. Collins was using that voice Mom and Dad used occasionally, one step below absolutely losing it. "That's enough. Quiet means quiet. I want to be able to hear a pin drop."

"Mo-*om*." Grace drew it out into two syllables.

"Even you, Grace. Pin. Drop."

What happens at Camp McSweeney stays at Camp McSweeney.

I wanted Austin to be right, but I had the worst feeling that this time he was so, so wrong.

CHAPTER THIRTEEN

By the time I stepped off the bus on Monday, my duffel might as well have been filled with bricks. That's how heavy it felt as I dragged it across the parking lot.

"Meow!" some boy shouted through a bus window.

"Mrooooowl."

"Hey!" Coach Lipinski shouted. "That's enough." He turned to Mrs. Haney, the social studies teacher, and in his thick Boston accent said, "I know it's always somethin' with kids this age, but I swear tah God, feels like we spent the weekend in an animal sheltah fulla stray cats."

I glanced back, searching for Becca. When I finally spotted her, she was looking down at the pavement, probably counting the seconds until she was safely home with her parents and away from all of us.

Up ahead, Mom and Dad stood beside Dad's Audi. Wait—why was Dad here? He was supposed to be on TV doing the six o'clock weather, not standing there in shorts and an old Red Sox T-shirt. I picked up my pace.

"Hey, Em. Did you have a good time?" Dad popped open the trunk.

"Why aren't you at the station?"

He pushed aside some sports equipment, ignoring my question as he made room for my bag. "How was the Cape?"

"Fine."

I took my place in the back seat, trying to figure it all out. Dad didn't get fired, did he? They wouldn't fire the most popular weather guy . . . right? As Dad navigated us out of the parking lot, I kept a close eye on Mom in the rearview mirror. She wasn't wearing any makeup—not that she did often—and her eyes looked tired. And she kept doing this thing with her jaw, like she was tightening and loosening it, maybe even grinding her teeth.

Did they already know what happened at Camp McSweeney? Had Becca's mom called and told them?

Or did Dr. Grossman not even know yet? Camp McSweeney was a "cell phone–free environment" after all.

"So," Dad said while we waited at a stoplight, "did you bring home any free potato chips?"

At the end of the factory tour, everyone had gotten a free bag of Cape Cod–brand potato chips. Some kids were saving them, others tore right in, but then once the boys started popping the bags on the bus, Coach Lipinski had to collect them.

"No, sorry," I said.

"Everything okay, E?" Dad eyed me in the mirror. "You're awfully quiet."

I could ask the same question of you and Mom, I thought as I picked some dirt out of my fingernail. "I'm just tired," I said. "We didn't get a lot of sleep." At least that was true.

We pulled into the driveway right next to Mom's car. Austin's was gone.

"Where's Austin?" I asked, stepping out of the car.

Just as Mom was opening her mouth to answer me, Dad cut in, his tone suddenly serious. "Emma, let's go have a chat in the living room."

Something had to be wrong, because Mom and Dad forgot about my bag in the trunk. This wasn't about what had happened with Becca, and Dad hadn't lost his job. The only time I'd ever heard about people having a "talk" in the living room was when their parents were getting divorced. But if that was happening, wouldn't Austin be here for it? Suddenly it occurred to me that maybe Austin's absence was on purpose.

Dad sat in his favorite leather chair while Mom took a seat on the sofa beside me. I picked at a thread dangling from my shorts. "Where's Austin?" I asked again. "Is he okay?" The worst thought flitted into my mind. Did he get into a car accident while I was gone? Was he dead? No, *no*. He couldn't be. They were too calm for that.

"Your brother's at an appointment," Dad said.

"With a counselor," Mom added.

A counselor. What kind? Since when?

But before I had a chance to ask any of those questions out loud, Mom continued. "While you were at school on Friday, I—" She sucked in a sharp breath and pinched the skin at the top of her nose. "I went in Austin's room. It had gotten so bad in there lately, I just wanted to clean up the place, let in some fresh air. But while I was tidying up, I found something. Emma, your brother's been taking painkillers—abusing opioid painkillers."

"He still had pills from his surgery? But that was all the way back in December."

"You're right," Dad said. "That prescription ran out a long time ago."

"But I don't get it." I shook my head. None of this made any sense. "Where was he getting pills from? And why? His shoulder's better. He's better. Right?" Mom's eyes filled with tears, and for a moment she couldn't answer me. "Dad?"

"Austin's addicted to them." He stared down at the carpet. "These opioid painkillers, they're very, very powerful."

"So why did the doctor give them to him in the first place?"

"Emma, it's complicated," Dad said. "We didn't think the amount he got after the surgery was enough to lead to . . . anything like this." He held his face in his hands for a moment. "But the problem is, he's well past that prescription now. He's been finding them other ways."

Other ways? What other ways? Like . . . like a drug dealer? Had my brother met up with drug dealers? This was like something out of D.A.R.E., back in first quarter, before we switched to art class. Police officers came into health class and told us all about drugs and how bad they were. But the way they talked about it, the videos they showed us? It never seemed like anything anyone I knew could ever, ever, ever do. Especially Austin.

"I don't understand. Tell me. Is this why . . . why . . . ?" But I couldn't say it. My lips and tongue didn't work right; they refused to form the question I wanted to ask.

Because I already knew the answer.

This was why Austin was changing. This was why everything had been different since his breakup with Savannah. His grades. His moods. All that time he spent in his room. Everything.

That sinking feeling I had, the one that came and went, it had been telling me something. Telling me that things with my brother were not okay. That feeling was right. Spot-on. But I'd ignored it.

"So what happens now?" I asked, needing something real to cling to.

"Dad and I have been very busy the past few days making calls and trying to figure this out," Mom said. "All of this is still so new. We've got a lot of catch-up to do, and we can't wait around."

"What do you mean?"

"Most of the nearby rehab facilities are full, with long waiting lists. We're hoping we can pull some strings and find a thirty-day facility with a room for Austin."

A *room* for Austin.

"You're sending him away?" I looked from Dad to Mom and back again. She had to be kidding. He didn't need to go away. Go away . . . where? How far?

"Only for a month," Dad said.

"But what about school?"

"One thing at a time, Em." Mom rested a hand on my bare knee. Her palm was cool to the touch, sending a shock up my leg. "Besides, you only have a few days left."

"This is a lot to process." Dad reached into his

pocket for a stick of gum, though he didn't put it in his mouth, just bent the piece back and forth, back and forth, until it broke in two. "You probably have a lot of questions. Mom and I will do our best to answer them, but if you want to see a counselor, like Austin is right now, we can set up an appointment. We're lucky: there's a wonderful psychologist in Cambridge who specializes in substance abuse and helping family members cope."

Helping family members. Me? Dad thought I needed help—*we* needed help—because of Austin? Everything was happening too fast, except also in slow motion. As if that made any sense. But then, nothing made any sense. Austin didn't have problems with drugs. No, this was all some kind of sick joke. A really, really messed-up joke.

Mom leaned toward me. "Emma? What are you thinking, hon? This conversation has been too one-sided."

I couldn't think anymore. I didn't want to think. I just wanted to go to bed. Lie down and close my eyes and fall deep asleep. I wanted to wake up and find out that none of this had happened. Not today, or the day before, or the day before that. I wanted to wake up and be a fifth grader again.

"I'm really tired," I said finally. "Can I go to my room and lie down?"

Mom caught Dad's eye. "You know, a nap sounds pretty good right about now. Mind if I join you?"

It'd been years since Mom had slept on my bed with me. According to Austin, she did it a lot when I was little. Supposedly I used to be afraid of the dark, but I'll be honest, I don't remember that and maybe he was making it up to mess with me.

"Sure," I said.

"Do you want me to grab your duffel out of the car, E?" Dad asked.

"I don't need it right now," I replied. And then we started up the stairs, just me and Mom.

My bed was only a twin, but Mom was tall and thin, and, like Lucy, she was good at squeezing into small spaces. I kicked off my shoes and lay down on the bed, facing the door. Mom climbed on behind me, slowly settling into place, her breath warm on the back of my neck. She reached out to undo my ponytail and stroke my hair, combing it with her fingers.

My hair still smelled like smoke from the campfire last night. When I closed my eyes, I could almost see Becca across the way, sitting all by herself. *Meow.*

They were so awful to her. I was so awful.

My pillowcase grew wet with tears, my nose so thick with snot I had to breathe through my mouth.

"I know, honey. I know," Mom whispered.

But she didn't. She didn't know at all. She only thought she knew.

It wasn't just those girls in the cabin that knew now. And I guess I should have realized that the second we started playing that stupid, stupid game with Grace Collins and Haven Mulligan. The whole sixth grade knew. And starting tomorrow, when we returned to school with everyone else, it would only get worse.

"Oh, my girl," Mom said. "I always thought I was so lucky. I had these two kids and they were so, so good. Such good kids. Not that you and Austin never gave me something to worry about. But it was never anything big. Never anything like . . ." She sniffled. "At least I don't have to worry about you."

Her saying that only made me cry harder.

I couldn't tell her the truth: that I was about as

far from a good kid as you could get. I'd covered for Austin that night when he sneaked out, when he was grounded back in late March. Had he gone out to buy drugs then? I should have said something to Mom and Dad, even if it made Austin mad at me. Never mind what happened with Becca. For three straight days, they'd humiliated her. All because of me and my big mouth.

No, telling Mom any of this would only make things worse. I needed to let her believe this about me. That I was a good kid.

Even if it was a lie.

CHAPTER FOURTEEN

When I finally woke up a few hours later, it was dark outside and the space beside me on the bed was empty. Downstairs, I heard voices in the kitchen. Mom's, Dad's, Austin's.

So he was back now.

From my desk I grabbed my iPhone and crawled back into bed, this time under the covers. I wasn't ready to go downstairs yet—not ready to see Austin. I still had so many questions.

But when I woke my phone up, I saw messages covering the whole screen.

From Kennedy, I'm sorry. I didn't mean it to come out like that. Can we just talk?

And Lucy. Emma, please write back. There's something I think could help.

None from Becca, though I opened my text thread with her and swiped down, down, down. All those times this spring when she wanted to hang out but I was busy with Kennedy and Lucy stared back at me. She was the one I needed to text. *I'm so sorry, Becs. I'm the worst. I don't even know why I said anything.*

But I couldn't bring myself to text half of that. Anything, really. What if she didn't forgive me? I couldn't take that on top of everything with Austin.

I opened up the web browser. What was that word my parents had used to describe the kind of painkillers Austin had taken after the surgery? The kind he'd somehow found for himself. Opie-something? When I typed it into the search bar, the word "opioid" popped up. That was it.

My eyes still puffy, I scrolled through article after article. The smell of chicken tikka masala wafted up through the floor vents, and I could hear the clanging of pots and pans from downstairs in the kitchen as I flipped back to the search page and saw a headline that made my stomach drop.

OPIOIDS COULD KILL NEARLY 500,000 IN THE US IN THE NEXT DECADE

Could Austin *die*?

My pointer finger trembled as I clicked on the article. I'd read only the first few paragraphs when there was a knock on my door. Out of surprise I dropped my phone on my lap. "Mom sent me to check on you. It's almost dinnertime."

That was all he had to say to me?

I leaped up from my bed, surprised by the energy that suddenly filled my body as I whipped open the door and pummeled my brother. "How could you be so stupid? *Drugs?* Austin, what's wrong with you?"

"Em," he said, his voice breaking.

"Where did you go that night? I covered for you."

"Emma, it's not your—"

"Where did you go? Where?"

From downstairs, Dad this time. "Dinner!"

I stared my brother down. "You have to tell me."

Austin raised his voice. "No, E. I don't." He slammed his fist against the wall, so hard I was surprised he didn't break through it. He cursed—not at me, though. At himself. His whole face crumpled like a used paper lunch bag. I'd never seen my brother like this. Not ever. "I'm sorry. I'm sorry. I'm sorry, okay? What else do you want me to say?"

"That you're not going to die." The words came out of my mouth before I had time to consider what saying them out loud to Austin right then would do.

The quiet in the hallway was overwhelming as Austin held his head in his hands. A million seconds passed. "That won't happen," he finally said.

But when I caught his eyes, they looked so dead. Like he didn't have any faith in the words coming out of his mouth either.

All I could think about were those articles I'd read online. And that number. Five hundred thousand. Already, over a hundred people had died from opioid overdoses in Massachusetts just this year. Did he know? If he did, how could he have ever done this? How could he have started?

Mom was right. He should have never played football.

I stomped back into my room.

"So, are you coming down?" he finally said, his voice calmer now, as if all this fuss was about dinner. Who could even think about eating? "What should I tell Mom and Dad?"

"You're pretty good at lying—you figure it out." I slammed the door behind me, my heart in my throat, and climbed back into bed.

I got it now, why Mom and Dad were sending him away. That article made it clear. Austin needed a restart. He needed to get away from everything that reminded him of the person he'd become the past six months.

"Emma?" It was Dad who came up, Dad who knocked on my door, letting himself in before I'd even said he could. But then, I guess we were done with that now. Austin had blown their trust, blown it for the both of us.

"Emma, we'd really love to have you at the dinner table." Dad sat at the edge of my bed.

"I'm not hungry."

"I know." He squeezed my feet through the covers. "Your mom and I haven't been that hungry the past few days either. And you know that's saying a lot for both of us. But we have to stick together. We're a family."

"Are you mad at him too?"

"I've wrestled with a whole lot of feelings the past few days. It probably wasn't the worst thing for you to have been away. I'll be honest, Em, we're all just trying to do our best right now. And for me that means trying to understand Austin and what he's been going through. Addiction is a disease. It's not a choice Austin made—it's chemical. And it's caused him to behave in ways that aren't like him. All this time he's been struggling with this on his own, but from now on, it's a team effort. You know your brother; he's always at his best when he's part of a team. With help, I believe he can beat this. And we're working very hard to get him the absolute best help out there."

A team effort.

"What do you say? Do you think you could come down and join us?"

I didn't think I could do it, sit at the table with my brother like everything was going to be fine. So I lied. "I think my stomach's a little upset," I said. "From the long bus ride. Can I come down for some cereal in a bit?"

"Sure thing, E." Dad pulled down my shades before leaving the room.

He left the door ajar on his way out, and for a while I just lay there listening to the three of them downstairs. The clinking of silverware against the plates. I couldn't remember such a quiet dinner in my house. Used to be, Dad would have some silly story from work—the sportscaster Mike was always up to something. And Mom usually had a billion questions for me and Austin about what had happened at school. And Austin would be filling them in about practice or a track meet. Used to be, I was the quietest one there. Just listening to all of them, or trying to open my mouth in time to share a story from school.

In the shadows of the hallway, I could almost see Austin as he stood there when I told him my biggest fear. I shouldn't have ever said it out loud. It was too big, too scary. Not just for me, but for him.

And that look in his eyes when he replied? Like the person he was the most angry with was himself?

I wanted to forget that more than anything, but I was afraid I couldn't.

CHAPTER FIFTEEN

Mom dropped me off at school Tuesday. She said I didn't have to go if I didn't want to, but the last place I wanted to be was home with her and Austin. I could still barely look at him. Plus, I had to get through only three more days and then we'd be out for summer.

Kennedy and Lucy were waiting for me by my locker. For once Kennedy wasn't her bouncy Tiggery self. More like Eeyore. "Emma," she said. "Please. Can we talk?"

Down the hall, I could hear it starting up again. "Meow? Meoooowwww." A math teacher popped his head out into the hallway and yelled, "Enough of that!" He muttered, "Kids these days."

"Emma?"

"No," I blurted back. "We can't. I have a lot going on right now and—" I remembered the name Mom had given me, of the counselor at school. Mrs. Dwyer. Mom had said she'd call her first thing and if I needed a place to go, any time, I could hang out there. "I have to go," I said. "Sorry."

I pushed past them and into the crowded hallway as the bell rang to signal five minutes till homeroom. I would survive the next three days, even if it meant spending my lunch periods in the counselor's office.

As I was packing up my backpack at the end of the day, Lucy stopped by my locker. I couldn't remember a time I'd ever hung out with just Lucy. Even when Kennedy was out sick for a few days this winter, Lucy was too—and it was strange seeing her without her other half.

"Hey," she said.

"Hey."

I was about to tell her I had to run when I realized that wasn't fair. Lucy wasn't Kennedy. She hadn't told the entire grade about Becca's kitty blanket. She was just best friends with the person who had.

"Have you seen her?" she asked.

At first I thought she meant Kennedy, but then I realized she meant Becca.

"Not today, no."

I wasn't sure if Becca had even come to school. After everything that happened, I figured the last person she wanted to see was me, so I hadn't tried to walk to school with her. It was a C day, which meant she had math at the high school. Maybe she'd gone straight there?

"Oh." Lucy grew quiet, but she didn't leave. There was clearly something else she wanted to say, but if she didn't say it soon, she'd be saying it to my locker because I had track practice. Well, not really much of a practice since all the meets were over. But the coach wanted us to get together for one last run as a team. "Ken really didn't mean this—any of it. She feels so bad, Emma. Please, hear her out."

"*She* feels bad? Look, I get it, but I'm sorry, I have to go."

I left her there and jogged down the hall and stairs, almost tripping over them a few times.

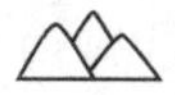

As I walked back home after track, all I could think about was the RISD summer camp in July. Two whole weeks at Lucy's grandma's place with her and Kennedy. I didn't think I could do it, but Mom and Dad had already sent in the deposit, and if I told them I didn't want to go anymore, they'd want to know why, and then I'd have to tell them about everything that happened at Camp McSweeney, and everything before. And I couldn't.

They were already worried about Austin. They didn't have any room left to worry about me.

I was almost home when I heard footsteps behind me, like someone was closing in on me. I was used to that sound from track—I got passed *a lot*—but it didn't usually happen when I was walking. I looked over my shoulder and was startled to see Becca there.

"What?" she said as my eyes caught hers. "You going to meow at me too?"

"Becca, I would never."

"You *told* her. Why would you do that?"

"I'm sorry, Becs. It was an accident. I—"

"An *accident*? How? How do you accidentally tell someone about that? It wasn't and you know it. You might as well own it." She crossed her arms.

"Well, the whole thing wouldn't have even happened if you'd just grow up like everyone else."

Her face right then, it looked like I'd hit her. And I guess I had, only with words.

Becca, I didn't mean it. But those words got lodged in my throat. Why did that keep happening to me? Why was it so, so hard to say the things I needed to say? There were so many other words stuck in there with them. Things I should've said to Mom, Dad, Austin, Kennedy. I was all clogged up.

She marched away from me in her too-big T-shirt and those shorts that looked like something my dad would wear, too long and cargo. Sometimes it felt like she did it on purpose. Like every part of her was some revolt against middle school.

It was my fault *and* it was her fault. And Kennedy's. It was everyone's fault. And I had no idea how to fix any of it.

When I was finally safe in my own house, I heard Mom on the phone in the kitchen. "You really think this could work? Oh, Delia, you're a lifesaver. Let me talk it over more with Tony tonight. I'll—great—

sounds good—I'll be in touch." She raised her voice. "E? Is that you?"

Mom's eyes lit up as she rounded the corner. "Oh, such an abundance of good news today. Finally. We found an abstinence-only rehab center that will take Austin and—" She stopped midsentence when she saw my face. "Everything okay, hon?"

"It's fine. I'm fine."

"Emma. You sure?"

"Just a weird day," I lied. "Saying goodbye to my C-day teachers and stuff." I pasted on a smile. I had to, right? I was part of the team and the team was doing well today. I had to be on the same page as the rest of my teammates.

"In any case, I made an appointment for that counselor in Cambridge for tomorrow right after school. That sound good to you?"

"Sure."

I kept my happy face on for the next fifteen minutes, following Mom into the kitchen while she got out some cheese and crackers and cut vegetables for us to snack on. When Mom decided to go for a run, I grabbed my phone and flipped through the text messages, not sure how to respond to any of them.

I wanted to be able to tell someone what was going on. Not some stranger I'd never met before, like that counselor I'd see tomorrow. A friend. But I couldn't trust Kennedy and Lucy, not after what had happened at Camp McSweeney. They couldn't keep a secret, and that's what this was. At least, I thought so. Mom and Dad hadn't said either way, but it felt like a secret.

But Becca, she could keep a secret. And Becca loved Austin like a brother.

But I couldn't tell her now. No, I'd ruined what we used to have. Possibly forever.

CHAPTER SIXTEEN

The following afternoon, Mom sat across from me at the new Froyo place in Harvard Square. "I'd like to talk to you about an idea Dad and I had—for you, for this summer."

I stared into my melty froyo. Clearly I'd left my appetite back at Camp McSweeney. "For me?"

"Delia and her husband, Chris, offered to have you come stay with them in Wyoming for the summer. They're both really excited to host you, that is, if you're up for it. It could be an adventure."

She was shipping me off to Wyoming to spend the summer with strangers. "Mom, I don't even know them." I stabbed my spoon hard into my frozen yogurt and left it there. She wasn't serious, was she?

"That's not true, Em."

"The last time I saw them I was wearing a *diaper*." In the back office of Happy Feet, Mom had this framed picture up on the wall of me and Sadie, her best friend's daughter, who's around my age. We were holding hands and spinning in the grass. Sadie's hair was dark brown and short, mine that shade of white blond that's gone by kindergarten. If you looked close, you could spot the blueberry stains on our shirts and our mouths.

But that picture was from a million years ago. We were just little kids. Mom and Delia, her best friend from college, used to get together more back then. Before our lives got so busy.

"I know it's been a while, but gosh, at this point Delia's heard so many stories about you, she feels like she practically knows you, Em. And she's so excited to have you. They all are. We always talked about a big summer road trip to Wyoming. . . ."

A *family* road trip, I wanted to remind her. With all four of us. Not just me, heading out on a plane by myself across the country to spend my summer with three people I barely remembered while everything back home was falling apart. Could I really leave them? Be that far away? What if something bad happened?

I slurped up some froyo, trying to think this all over. "But what about camp?"

Mom's shoulders shot up as she took in a deep breath. "About that, hon . . . The timing would be really tricky with everything going on with Austin. It's smack in the middle of the summer. I know it's something you and your friends have been looking forward to for so long, but I just . . ." She hesitated, probably waiting for me to flip my lid.

Sure, it stung, thinking I would miss out on the two weeks at RISD I'd been looking forward to for months. But right now I couldn't imagine two weeks of nonstop Kennedy. I could still barely look at her after what she did.

This trip, though. It could be my excuse.

"When would I leave?" I asked.

"Ideally on Friday." She grimaced.

My eyes went wide. "*This* Friday?"

"It's sooner than I'd like too, Em, believe me. But the demand for these beds is so high right now. And we've got to get Austin in somewhere. If we can get you to Logan Friday morning, we'll get Austin down to the Cape in time."

I wanted Austin to get help as soon as possible. "What can I tell Lucy and Kennedy, then? About Austin, I mean."

"Dad and I still have to figure that out. For now, how about you leave that to us. One of us will give their parents a call in a few days, once we've figured out what to say. Do you think you can keep quiet for now? Is that too much to ask?" She rubbed her eye, and for a minute I thought she was going to start crying in public.

"Mom, it's okay. It's okay. I won't say anything. It's not that hard. Really." And the truth was, it wouldn't be. How hard could it be not to tell anyone when I wasn't really talking to any of them?

Mom's face crumpled. "You've been such a champ the past few days, Em. I really don't know what Dad and I would do without you."

I didn't know what to say to her. A champ? If only she knew who I really was.

For the last day of school, all I could think about was Wyoming. And that was sort of weird because I didn't know one thing about Wyoming. When I heard the word, I only thought of cowboys and that big national park with the geysers—but was that Yellowstone or Yosemite? I always got them mixed up.

The night before, Mom kept telling me what a blast it'd been when she lived there one summer in college, and it was funny because I couldn't picture Mom in Wyoming at all. There was too much Boston in her. She'd survived a whole summer without Dunkin' and the Red Sox and early-morning swims in Walden Pond? Really? If you say so.

During lunch I spent most of the time in Mrs. Dwyer's office before heading to the cafeteria at the very end of the period. For a second there I thought Kennedy was going to choke on her roll as I slid in across from her.

"I can't come to the camp anymore," I said. Though my voice sounded almost robotic, I was surprised by the little pinch that came when I heard those words float out of my mouth. That thing I'd been looking forward to for months was gone. Over. Done.

"Emma, no." Lucy started to tear up, and for a second I felt so bad I considered pulling her aside to tell her the truth: that it wasn't up to me.

"I'm going to Wyoming," robot-me said.

"Just you or your whole family?" Kennedy asked.

"Just me," I said, whipping that fake smile out of my back pocket. I'd gotten good at using it the past few days, so good I was starting to scare myself. Parroting Mom, I added, "It's going to be an adventure." But this time, when I said those words out loud, something strange happened. I almost believed them. "Isn't that what real artists do? They don't go to some kids art camp. They go somewhere new and explore, right? Anyway. Just wanted to let you know."

I got up from the seat, my heartbeat calming down with each step I took away from Kennedy and Lucy. I'd done the hard thing. I'd told them. The tiniest weight had been lifted from my shoulders. And now I was free.

"Emma, wait," Kennedy said, standing up, her mouth for once completely empty of rolls.

But I was already on my way.

The very next day, Dad would take me to the airport for the flight to Denver. Turns out the tiny airports out west are hard to fly into at the last minute, so Delia and Sadie and maybe even Delia's husband, Chris, were going to make the drive from their small town in northeastern Wyoming all the way into Denver for me. I wasn't totally buying Mom's "That's how excited they are to see you." More like, that was how bad they felt for my mom. Bad enough to spend ten hours round-trip in a car to pick me up.

I didn't really have a choice in the matter. The last thing Mom and Dad needed was a tantrum from Emma. Besides, ever since that moment in the cafeteria when I told Kennedy and Lucy my plan, I'd started to think maybe it could happen. Maybe Wyoming could be an adventure.

Once Dad dropped me off at the airport, he and Mom would drive Austin down to Cape Cod, to the closest abstinence-based rehab facility they could find that had good ratings *and* an open bed. He'd be there for thirty days, and then, at the end, if everything went well, they'd let him come home.

Home. That was the part Mom and Dad were most worried about. Austin would need to learn all over again how to have a real life, without any drugs.

My suitcase was laid out on my bed, packed with shorts and T-shirts, a bathing suit—did people even go swimming in Wyoming? There aren't any beaches, but there must be lakes, right? A pool? Plus jeans, my lucky sweatshirt, some long-sleeved shirts in case it got cold at night, and a dress in case we went somewhere fancy. Mom said we might go hiking, so I dug around in my closet for those hiking sneakers I'd gotten a few years ago when we went to New Hampshire for a week. Did they still fit?

Knock-knock.

I had them on both hands like mittens when I turned to see who it was.

Austin stood in the doorway with a hand in his pocket. He didn't look like a drug addict, at least not like the ones I'd seen around Harvard Square before, all spaced-out and skinny, dark circles under their eyes. Austin wasn't as tan as he used to be from being outside all afternoon at track practice, but his arms were still muscular. His hair had gotten so long he could tuck it behind his ears.

"Looks like you're ready to go," he said, stepping into my room.

I glanced at my suitcase. "I don't know if any of my clothes are *cool* for Wyoming."

"You probably need a cowboy hat. Or some boots."

"Yeah, that's what I need. Cowboy boots." I knew he was trying to be nice, but I couldn't. The whole thing still smarted.

He pulled his hand out of his pocket and handed me a piece of paper. When I unfolded it, I could see he'd scrawled out the address for the rehab center he'd be at. His handwriting had always been so bad, but I could still read it. At least, I was pretty sure.

"I'm not allowed to have my phone with me, but they said you can write. If you want, I mean."

"Austin."

He shook his head. "I should have never—I'm sorry, Em. I'm really—"

I didn't know what to say back to him. If he was really sorry, he would have stopped. If he was really sorry, I wouldn't be leaving for Wyoming tomorrow morning. If he was really sorry, he would have been there for me so I could have told him about what happened at Camp McSweeney and he would have helped me figure out how to make things right with Becca and what I was even supposed to do about Kennedy. Could I trust her again? Accept her apology?

But no. He wasn't around then, or the months before. Not really. He wasn't depressed—or maybe he was. He was high. He was on drugs. He didn't care about me or Mom and Dad. Just himself.

I reached down for my backpack and slipped the paper into the front pouch.

"Look, I know I've ruined your summer plans. What's Becca even going to do with you gone for the whole summer?"

Just hearing her name gave me another pang of guilt. But Austin didn't seem to notice that it took me a second to say, "She'll survive." I hoped that was true. At least now that school was out, she wouldn't have to listen to other kids taunting her with meows.

"Hey, I bet you'll find your people in Wyoming. They might wear cowboy hats and hang out with prairie dogs on the weekend, but they're there." He cracked a smile, trying to get me to follow. "Okay, guess I'd better pack. You're way better at it than I am, and if I don't finish soon, Dad's going to breathe down my neck even more."

Once he was back in his room, I zipped up my suitcase and set it on the floor. I wasn't sure Austin got what I was doing for him. Traveling across the country to stay with strangers for the entire summer so Mom and Dad could focus on him. Didn't he wonder why I wasn't more upset, more resistant? But then, he hadn't really been thinking about me or anyone else in this family for a while now, had he?

Maybe it'd finally occur to him while he's at rehab. He didn't just do this to himself. He did this to all of us.

From my desk I grabbed the sheet of paper Nisha had handed me when I passed by the art room right before lunch. She'd told me to share it with Kennedy and Lucy, but I couldn't. It was hard enough telling them I'd canceled on the camp.

The local arts council was running a contest for anyone ages twelve to eighteen, with a deadline of September 1. I'd have the whole summer to come up with something. What I'd said to Kennedy and Lucy in the cafeteria, I'd made up on the spot. I didn't exactly believe it. But maybe I was right. Maybe an artist really did need to get away to come up with something new.

I folded the sheet of paper into thirds and tucked

it into my backpack pocket, where it sat with Austin's address.

"How you making out, A?"

Austin wasn't kidding. Dad never took time off from the station unless it was a holiday or we were on vacation, but Mom didn't trust Austin unattended and she had some work to do at the store, so Dad was on duty. He must've set a timer on his phone, reminding him to check on Austin every fifteen minutes.

Was that how they'd be when the rehab center discharged Austin? Checking on him every fifteen minutes, watching him like he was a toddler? Would it be like that forever? Would we *ever* go back to normal?

Maybe it was okay that I was going to be in Wyoming and not here when Austin came back.

"All packed up?" Dad peeked his head in my room.

"Pretty much."

He half closed the door behind him. "I'm really impressed by how you've handled everything, E. You're really taking one for the team."

The team, again. So I was on the team. The best player, even. Then how come I felt like such a failure?

I'd failed Austin and Becca. And now I was running away from all of it. All the way to Wyoming.

"You're going to have so much fun out west. I just wish we could be with you. Maybe next summer. Promise to scout out all the good spots and report back?"

"Sure," I said, beaming back at Dad.

He kissed the top of my head. "That's my girl." He ran his hands through his hair. "All right, back to check on that brother of yours."

As he left, I grabbed my phone from the bedside table and started typing a message to Becca. I'm so sorry about everything. I'm leaving for Wyoming tomorrow. There's something I have to tell you. It's about Austin. Can we talk? Please.

But like all the other ones from the past few days, I deleted it instead of hitting send.

NOW

CHAPTER SEVENTEEN

We hit the ground with a big bump, the airplane's brakes squealing as we careen down the runway. Immediately I turn off airplane mode on my phone and text Dad. Landed.

From beneath the seat in front of me, I pull out my backpack and slide in the sketchbook with my failed attempt at a letter to Becca. As if a letter could somehow fix things. As if a letter could ever be enough.

I clutch my backpack to my chest as we taxi over to a gate. The guy next to me wakes up and slides his headphones off. "Visiting Denver?" he asks.

"Wyoming, actually."

"All by yourself? You're braver than me."

I doubt that and offer him a small shrug. He doesn't ask what brings me out this way. Even if he did, I'm not sure what I'd tell him. The truth? Part of the truth? Or some white lie, made up on the spot?

When we land, I'm met by my escort, a short young woman named Jessica with long shiny black hair. We walk for what feels like forever, eventually passing by a store selling purple-and-gray Colorado Rockies T-shirts, and that's when I feel it, feel it for real. How far I am from Boston, from my family, from everyone I know.

It's like my parents traded me to another team for the summer. Another family. I haven't even been gone twenty-four hours—I can't be homesick. Not yet.

We take the escalator down to the train toward baggage claim, and while we're on it, I get a text from my dad. *Let us know when you've found Delia. Love you.* The train comes to a stop, and I shove my phone into my backpack. At baggage claim I start looking for them—Delia; her husband, Chris; and Sadie. Mom wasn't sure if all three of them would make the drive, but she hoped Sadie would tag along.

The thing is, I don't even know who I'm looking for exactly. They used to send us Christmas cards every year with a photo of the three of them. Mom'd tack it on the fridge with one of her bajillion 26.2 magnets. The photo was always of something exciting they'd done that year—an African safari or a baseball game in Tokyo. Delia's a teacher, so she gets summers off, which always makes Mom jealous. She says some summer she'll trust Betsy to run the store and Dad'll take a sabbatical from the station, but who is she kidding? Not me.

"Emma?"

Standing by the ATM is a tall, tan woman in yoga pants, her short curly brown hair kept back by a headband. I search her face and see a glimmer of the woman from the Christmas cards. Finally someone I know! Well, sort of.

I say goodbye and thank you to Jessica and head to Delia, who wraps me tight in a bear hug. "So great to see you, kid. I can't believe how long it's been. Too long. Way too long." She takes a step back. "Oh, Emma, you look so much like your mom."

"Really?" No one ever says that back home. They

always say I look like Dad. His build, his eyes, his complexion. That Austin's all Mom. Athletic and fidgety, always needing to be busy. The only thing I got from Mom was my hair, thick and blond and way more of it than I can handle.

"Oh, so much, kid." She whips around. "Darn it. Where'd Sadie wander off to now?" Delia pats my arm. "Probably needed to charge her phone again. Let's go grab your suitcase."

We head to the conveyor belt and quickly spot my bag. A teenage girl with long brown hair wearing cutoffs and a way-too-big tank top wanders over to us, chewing on the straw of a Starbucks frappé.

That's Sadie? I focus hard, trying to find pieces of that girl from the picture way back when, but I can't. I see bits of Delia in her, though. The same nose and posture.

Sadie turns to me. "So you're . . . Emily?"

"Sadie!" Delia sighs. "Sorry, Emma. She knows your name; she just has a weird sense of humor."

"Oh," I say. Already I like Delia, but I'm not so sure about Sadie. "Okay."

Sadie presses a finger to her temple. "Sorry, I've got

this raging headache right now, which hopefully the caffeine will fix. You drink coffee?"

I shake my head. What twelve-year-old drinks coffee?

"You're missing out."

"How . . . old are you?"

"I'll be fifteen in October."

Fifteen?

For a second my eyes well up. How could Mom not have said that? Sadie wasn't just a little bigger than me in the picture; she was *older*. More than two years older. It was one thing for a three-year-old and a five-year-old to play together because their moms were friends, but there's a huge difference between seventh grade and high school.

I hope that's the only key detail Mom left out.

We've got about forty-five minutes left on the drive to the town where Delia and Sadie live when something up the road catches my eye. Something huge and brown and . . .

"What's that up ahead?" I ask, pointing.

From the back seat Sadie says, "You mean the bison?"

As we get closer, I can see that's what they are. Bison. Buffalo? I don't know the difference, only that they're Austin's favorite animal. When he was little—before I came around, obviously—he had this stuffed animal he took with him everywhere. He called it his "buffy." By the time I was born, he'd outgrown it, but he was still obsessed with bison. I swear, the only reason he even likes that band Modest Mouse is because they have buffalo on all their stuff.

Now that I think about it, did Delia give him that stuffed animal?

I reach for my phone to text him, but then I remember he doesn't have his. Won't for a whole thirty days. "Are they always there like that? Just hanging out by the side of the road?"

Delia laughs. "Their terrain's a lot bigger. As far as you can see, out that way. Huge ranches in this part of the state."

Huge ranches. "Wait. People eat them?"

"Where'd you think bison burgers and bison jerky came from?" Sadie pipes up from the back seat.

"Oh."

Delia peeks in the rearview mirror to see if there's anyone behind us, but the highway out here is quiet—the complete opposite of Boston. She slows the car to a crawl as we pass them. There are five of them. Two big ones, three little. A family? The largest has clumps of fur falling off him like he's shedding. His head has got to be as big as my whole body. *Hey there*, I say in my head.

I take a quick video with my phone to share with Austin later. I want him to see them, just chilling by the side of the road.

"Kind of majestic, aren't they?" Delia says.

"Kind of smelly if you ask me."

Delia takes a hand off the steering wheel and playfully swats Sadie's knee.

We're past them now, but I watch in the side mirror as they get smaller and smaller until they're just a smudge of brown against the blue sky.

In the back seat Sadie cracks open a library book, and I can hear the spine breaking. Becca would kill her for that, if she were here. Call her a book murderer. She did that once to Ethan Shaw back in Mrs. Katsoulis's fourth-grade ELA class. The entire class cracked up, and it became an inside joke for the rest of the year.

Of course, that time they were laughing *with* Becca, not at her.

CHAPTER EIGHTEEN

When I pull up the shade in the guest room, the moon casts shadows on the wall. Delia's sewing machine, the pile of quilt squares, the old jam jar filled with pencils and markers and scissors. Something tells me most of their guests lately haven't been people so much as quilts.

My phone's still plugged into the wall outlet. When I grab it, the bright screen blinds me for a second. Five twenty-five.

I want to crawl back into bed, but I'm wide-awake.

Of course I am. Back home it's 7:25. Back home I'd be eating breakfast, getting ready to head to the store with Mom. Back home I'd—

I guess it doesn't matter what I'd be doing back home. I'm here now, right?

Still in my pajamas, I creep down the hallway. Delia's house is a split-level, and her former craft room/guest bedroom is on the lower level. Across the hall from me is Sadie's bedroom. The door is covered with posters for bands and Broadway musicals—*Hamilton*, *Dear Evan Hansen*, even *Cats*. This one band Lucy got obsessed with right before school ended is on there too. Just thinking about Lucy makes my stomach pinch. She texted me a bunch of times yesterday, but I still haven't responded.

It always felt like she and Kennedy shared one body, one brain. But I know she doesn't really. She's her own person. She didn't do what Kennedy did.

But there's no way to be friends with her without also being friends with Kennedy. Not even over text. I'm sure she'd tell Kennedy whatever I say. So I guess I shouldn't text back. At least, not yet.

I pad up the carpeted stairs to the living room. Their cat, Dumbledore, a fat gray thing with one fang sticking out, is curled up on the sofa, peering at me with glowing green eyes. I grab a glass of water from the kitchen sink and tiptoe over to him.

"Hey," I whisper.

I don't know why I wait for him to say something back. Of course he doesn't. *He's a cat, Emma.* Good grief.

I reach out cautiously, but he surprises me by leaning into my hand. I scratch under his chin. "Aw, hey, buddy." I stroke down his back and his tail, the only sound his purring and the ticking of the grandfather clock in the dining room. "You'll be my friend here, right?" I'm leaning down to rub my chin against the top of his head when he swipes my cheek with his paw.

"Oh, okay then."

Dumbledore hops off the couch, his tail sashaying with each step.

"So that's how it's going to be." I touch my cheek to see if he drew blood. Thankfully, no.

I'm about to go back downstairs for my sketchbook when I hear footsteps from the direction of Chris and Delia's bedroom. Chris comes in, still in his pajamas too. He's rubbing his beard and his dark brown hair sticks up in the back. "Thought I heard another early bird. Morning, Emma."

"Good morning."

"You always an early riser?"

I shake my head. "Not back home. I think it's the time change."

He pops into the kitchen and pulls a bottle of orange juice from the fridge. "You want some?" I nod and he pours me a glass, bringing it back to the living room. "Has Delia told you what I do for work?"

In the five-hour drive yesterday, Delia talked plenty, but I don't remember her mentioning that.

"I work at the mines, just outside of town."

"Oh."

"Do you know much about mines?"

"I used to play Minecraft . . . but I'm guessing it's not the same."

Chris laughs. "Not really." He explains how the whole reason anyone lives out in the middle of nowhere in Wyoming is because of the coal mines and that he works more than a mile underground. "I could take you down there sometime to see, if you'd like."

I don't even like being in basements. Without natural light or fresh air, I feel trapped. But I don't want to hurt his feelings, so I say, "Maybe?"

"Anyhow, the reason I wanted you to know is because my schedule's kind of peculiar. I work twelve-hour days, and then I get time off, and unfortunately you got here during one of those stretches where I'm at work a lot, so you may not see much of me for the rest of the week."

"That's okay," I say before realizing that sounds like I don't like him. "Sorry, I mean—"

"No worries. In any case, I'm sure Delia and Sadie can keep you entertained." He takes a sip of his orange juice, staring past me out the huge bay window. "We're so glad to have you here. We'd do anything for your mom. She's been through a lot lately with your brother."

I stare at the pile of magazines on the coffee table: *The Atlantic, Yoga Journal, Real Simple.* You can learn a lot about people from the magazines they leave lying around. Already I'm feeling better about not packing a cowboy hat.

"He's a good kid. I know he is because he came from your mom and dad. It's not easy being a teenager. Sometimes it feels like the whole world has changed since I was that age—and now as parents, Delia and I are just scrambling to keep up. Growing up in a mining town myself, I'm no stranger to substance abuse and all the hurt it can bring to a family. In any case, I just want you to know, if you ever want to talk about things, I'm happy to listen."

When Mom took me to see the counselor in Cambridge earlier this week, it was all new. I was still in so much shock, I barely knew what to say. Barely even knew what I thought. And I wasn't exactly ready to sit down in an office and talk about it with a complete stranger. But here, now, with Chris? It feels different. "*Your* family?" I ask.

"My father was an alcoholic."

"Oh," I say. "I'm sorry."

"Nothing for you to be sorry about," Chris says. "He was a complicated man. And I loved him very much. Just like you do Austin."

I chew on the inside of my cheek. It stops the tears from welling up in my eyes. Who am I to even think how weird it is to be in this nice house in Wyoming when Austin's in some treatment facility with no one he knows at all? I picture his room there—blank white walls, no Modest Mouse poster, no Patriots banner. And not even his cell phone to text a friend or me or Mom or Dad. He's entirely alone. Removed from everything—no, *everyone*—he's ever known.

"Emma?" Chris's voice startles me.

"Sorry."

"Emma, there's nothing to be sorry about. It's okay."

But he doesn't know. There's plenty to be sorry about. I should have said *something* to Mom and Dad. I could have stopped it. Maybe not entirely. But maybe if I'd said something, it wouldn't be this bad. Not so bad that Austin had to get sent away.

But I can't tell him any of this because he might tell Mom, and she still thinks I'm good. She needs to keep thinking that. Not worrying at all about me. I'm here, in this nice house. Chris is right. It's okay. It's okay—for me.

And okay has to be good enough.

I clear my throat. "Maybe we could talk about Austin some other time. I don't want to make you late for work."

"Whenever you're ready," Chris says. And then he excuses himself, leaving me all alone again.

Outside, the sun rises and I'm finally seeing Wyoming in daylight. Mom was right about one thing. The sky here *is* big. More than big. Endless.

When Sadie stops her bike in front of the library, I'm still panting from the past hour. Maybe Mom could keep up with Sadie, but even after an entire season of track, I barely can. At Delia's request, Sadie has spent this morning giving me an unofficial tour of town.

"And here," Sadie says as she hops off her bike, "is the library." She walks her bike over to the bike rack and locks it, and I follow suit. I'm still fumbling with the lock when Sadie sighs. "Come on!" she says, heading for the entrance.

Finally I get the lock to click and jog after her, out of breath all over again. Sadie stops outside the library's café. "When I told my mom I'd take you out, I completely spaced about meeting up with my friends. We've got this summer school project due next week, and this is the only time that worked for everyone. You don't mind hanging out here for a bit, do you?"

"No, no," I say. "That's totally fine. How long?"

"An hour? Maybe an hour and a half." She peeks into the café and waves at a group of girls circled around a table. "One sec," she shouts at them.

There's a sinking feeling in the center of my chest.

Sadie didn't want to give me this tour of town today. She *had* to. She didn't have a choice. I'm just this stranger thrust into her life for the summer. No warning, no nothing.

She's not going to be my buddy here for the summer. Maybe at first she'll pretend to her mom like she's trying, but it's not going to happen. She's got her own life, and she's not going to squeeze me into it. I'd be stupid to expect that.

"Text me when you're done?" I say, acting like everything's fine. It has to be, so it is.

I enter her number into my phone and she enters mine, and then she's off. And just like yesterday at the airport, again I'm on my own.

The library is spacious and modern, not at all like the library back home. That one is old enough to have a plaque outside saying it was built in the 1800s. Not that I really went there that much. The public library was on the other side of town, closer to where Kennedy and Lucy live. Actually, if I'd gone more, I probably would've met them earlier. From what Kennedy said, the teen librarian was super into anime like her and Lucy, and they even had an anime club for a few years.

Then again, I never exactly needed a library. Being friends with Becca was like having my own personal librarian.

At one of the computers, I search "bison" and write down the Dewey decimal numbers on a little card. It takes a while to locate the books, but nobody offers to help me, and actually, it's kind of nice to wander through the stacks until I find the books with the right numbers. I pull out a thick hardcover and wipe the dust off the top of it. *Bison: An American Icon.*

It's the kind of book Dad would pack for vacation. He always goes with nonfiction, the longer the better, even though his bookmark never seems to make it past the first quarter. He's too chatty for reading. Always busy gabbing with strangers or bugging the three of us.

I take the book over to the Teen Room, where there are two booths, a leather sofa, and several rolling shelves of books. It's cool and quiet, except for a librarian typing away. I settle into the leather sofa, open up the bison book, and start reading.

I don't know how long I've been sitting here when someone says, "You stole my seat," and I jump.

"S-s-sorry," I stammer.

"Whoa, whoa. I was kidding. You don't have to move." It's a boy about my age. He's wearing white pants and a black T-shirt with a quote from Harry Potter, I SOLEMNLY SWEAR THAT I AM UP TO NO GOOD. His curly brown hair is the littlest bit messy, kind of how Chris's looked this morning, but more like he made it that way on purpose. "I've never seen you here before. You new?"

There's something about the way he talks that's different, but I can't put my finger on it. "I guess."

"You're either new or you're not. There's not really much to guess."

It's an accent, I realize. Kind of countryish? Except Delia, Chris, and Sadie don't have one.

"Fine, then. You got me. I'm new."

"Knew it," he says, raising his eyebrows. He slips a bookmark into his book and reaches out a hand. "I'm Tyler."

"Emma."

"Emma," he repeats. "From . . . ?"

"Oh, right." I laugh. "Boston."

"Emma from *Baw-ston*. Did I do it right?"

“That accent?” I shake my head. “Not exactly.”

“So, what the heck are you even doing out here, then, Emma from Baaaah-ston. No offense, but people from Boston don’t usually hang out in this corner of Wyoming.”

“My parents wanted me to have an adventure,” I say. It’s not a lie, exactly. He doesn’t need to know how last-minute this trip really is. For all he knows, this trip was planned out months in advance. Some kind of cultural exchange. Transplant the East Coast girl into wild Wyoming and see how it takes.

“Your parents wanted you to have an adventure?”

“Are you pretty much going to repeat what I say?”

“Am I pretty much—oh no. You’re right. I’m totally doing it.” We both start laughing.

“Shhhh!” Across the way, the librarian has a finger to her lips and a scolding look on her face.

“Don’t worry about her,” Tyler says. “Stephanie’s harmless.”

“You sure?” If you ask me, she sort of looks like she wants to kick us out of here. I know that look, even if I’m not usually the one who gets it.

“I practically live here.” He must see the look on my

face as I try to figure out what that means. "*Practically*. Not literally. And not the fake 'literally' that people use all the time. Anyway, I do have a home. Oh my gosh, you need to get around Wyoming more. We're not all hicks, you know. Well, okay, some of us are."

I have a feeling this boy would just keep on talking whether I was here or not. He and Kennedy could have a contest. "I don't think that," I say.

"Good."

My phone buzzes with a text from Sadie. We're done. Where are you? How did an hour and a half go by so fast? I stand on my tippy toes so I can see the library entrance, and sure enough, she's there, waiting for me.

"Crap," I say, my finger still holding the place in my book. "I can't check it out. I don't have a card yet."

"You can use mine."

"Really?"

Tyler flashes me a thumbs-up. "You'll return it in three weeks, right? You've already read a third of it."

But you barely know me.

"Well?" he says.

I'm not sure what to do. He trusts me. We've been

talking for only ten minutes and already he's treating me like . . . like a friend. He probably shouldn't. He doesn't know what he's getting himself into.

"Come on." Tyler reaches his hand out for the book. "I'll take it to Stephanie. She'll check it out for me. I've got an in with her. Big-time."

An *in* with the librarian? What is he, the male version of Becca? Except, no. He's weirdly self-confident. Becca would never be this way with a stranger our age.

"You sure?"

"For the billionth time, yes."

By the time Sadie comes over, the bison book is back in my hand with a little printed slip tucked inside. "Of course you would find a book about bison. You're really obsessed, huh?"

I shrug.

"See you around," Tyler says. Just then I catch the cover of the book in his hand. *Boy Meets Boy.* The words are inside little candy hearts.

It doesn't *necessarily* mean he's gay, I tell myself. Still, I wonder.

As we head for the exit, I ask Sadie, "So what's your project?"

"Just this math thing. Nothing exciting."

As I unlock my bike, I can't stop myself from comparing Sadie to Austin. I just want to get to know her a little, but she's so closed off. With Austin, any question is like an open invitation for him to ramble on about who knows what. At least that's how it used to be.

But then again, he's my brother. And Sadie? She doesn't have to open up to me. We're not anyone to each other.

CHAPTER NINETEEN

When Sadie and I get back to the house, we find the kitchen table covered with maps and travel books. "I've got an idea," Delia says with a grin.

Sadie snags an apple from the fruit bowl and mumbles, "Oh great," before biting into it with a snap.

"You haven't even heard it yet." Delia pretends to be insulted and turns to me. "I bet Emma here keeps an open mind. Right?"

Before I have a chance to answer, Sadie sneaks in another quip. "That's because she's not your daughter."

"Oh, stop it already, Sades. Enough with the suspense. Here is my idea." Delia stretches her hands out for the official announcement. "A girls-only camping trip!"

"Can I bring some friends?" Sadie asks, although with her mouth full of apple it sounds more like "Can I brih suh fruhz?"

Delia furrows her brow. "*We're* the girls. Us three."

Sadie eyes me and her mom before swallowing. "Oh."

"Oh, come on. We don't have to go far. Just the Bighorns. Emma's never been. All of this is new to her. What do you say, Em?"

I'm torn between pleasing Delia and appeasing Sadie. "That sounds fun," I say. "But I don't mind if one of Sadie's friends wants to come along. . . ."

Delia bats that suggestion away. "There's plenty of time for Sadie to hang out with her friends all summer. But we've only got two months with you. Let's make 'em count, kiddo." She squeezes my shoulder. "You like camping, right?"

I have a feeling there's only one correct answer to this question. "Suuuure." In truth, we O'Malleys haven't camped since that one time when I was in third grade. Our first mistake was trying to cram all four of us into one tent. Evidently I kept kicking Austin in the night. And then I woke up in the middle of the night having to pee but was too afraid to walk to the restrooms and may have wet my sleeping bag and—yeah, beyond that I've blocked out the rest of the camping trip.

"Great!" Delia claps her hands together. "Oh, and I just finished this article in *Real Simple* about unplugging, and I think to truly experience nature, we're going to have to leave the cell phones at home."

"Mom, no," Sadie says.

"Only for a couple nights. We'll get back into town just in time for your summer school class on Tuesday. It'll be good for all of us. We're all, myself included, far too addicted to—" The second that word comes out, she winces. "Oh, Emma." She turns to me, her mouth in this puckered pity frown, and I want to evaporate. No, really. I want to turn into air, be invisible.

Aside from the conversation with Chris this morning, no one's said anything about Austin. But I guess I knew that couldn't last.

"It's okay," I tell Delia.

"No, it isn't. I'm sorry, Em. We use these words so carelessly sometimes, not thinking what they truly mean to people."

Sadie stands there uncomfortably, twisting the stem on the apple core. What does she think about Austin? Does she judge him—me, my parents? She sets the apple core on the table and snags her phone out of her pocket, proving Delia's point.

"When would we leave?" I ask, eager to change the subject.

"In an hour or so? We'd get in just in time for dinner. How does that sound?"

"Like I have a choice," Sadie mutters, scooping up the apple core and chucking it in the nearby trash can. It hits the bottom with a clang, and then she retreats downstairs, resigned to tagging along on this trip.

"Don't worry about her," Delia says, once Sadie's out of earshot. "She's still adjusting to everything. We'll have fun, the three of us. You'll see." Her earnest smile makes me think it's still possible. In any case, the decision's not mine to make. I'm just a guest here.

I excuse myself and head downstairs with my library book. Worry about Sadie? Why would I waste any time worrying about Sadie?

No, her reaction makes perfect sense. I only wonder why Delia doesn't see it. Maybe she feels indebted to my mom in some way, enough to help out, but Sadie's got nothing to do with it.

There's no space left in my mind to be concerned about Sadie when there's so much to worry about with Austin. If Mom and Dad think putting two thousand miles between me and Austin will stop the worrying, they're crazy. In some ways, the distance only makes it worse.

The door to Sadie's room is closed now, but I can hear her talking. Probably complaining to her friends about how her mom's dragging her on a camping trip. She's got music playing in the background, but every so often her voice cuts through the sound.

I close the door behind me and sit at the edge of my bed. I check my phone, as if somehow I've missed one of the many, many text messages coming from back home. I wish. What I wouldn't give for a text message from Becca right now. Even an angry one.

No, Emma. Stop. Stop right now.

My eyes smart, but I stop myself short of giving in to a pity party.

The strange thing is, even though I hear Sadie's voice coming from across the hall, somehow I can still imagine the knock on my door and my brother letting himself in, his hair damp from the shower. How I'd end up elbowing him as he made fun of me for something stupid.

Austin just talking to me. The way he used to. I want to hear it: his voice, his stories. The funny ones, the complainy ones, even the random ones that don't really have a point.

What if that never happens again? No, really. I read all those stories online. About people whose moms or dads or brothers or sisters can't ever get it together and float in and out of their lives. About how things seem like they're okay for a while, and then—blam—they're not.

Addicted to a cell phone?

As if it's at all the same.

The inside of my cheek is firmly latched between my teeth.

No, no, no.

That can't be Austin. It can't. It won't. I suck in a deep breath. And another. And another.

No, this rehab thing is going to work. Mom and Dad, they said it was the best one. They said how fortunate it was for Austin that a spot opened up just when he needed it. And they caught this early, right?

Thirty days off drugs is going to fix him. Help him go back to the person he was before. Like a reset. A rewind. All the way back to last fall, before any of this happened.

Maybe Austin can't technically do his junior year over. Not at school, at least. But he can start over. He can go back.

God, he's got to.

I reach for my backpack, pull out my sketchbook, and begin making lists about Austin, how he used to be. How he can be again.

And the objects that define him: the buffalo stuffed animal, his favorite UCLA T-shirt, that beat-up paperback of *Slaughterhouse-Five* he tore through last summer on the Cape and declared to be the best book he'd ever read.

And by the time I'm done, I feel better. Almost like I put all my worries about Austin in a box and shut the lid.

I put the sketchbook and buffalo book into my

backpack and head upstairs to see what Delia's up to and how I can help get ready for the camping trip.

When I ask Delia where the Bighorns are, she says they're in the next town up the road. The next town. Close by, right?

Not in Wyoming. Turns out if you head north from here, the next town, Buffalo, is two hours away.

Two. Hours.

You drive that far in one direction in Massachusetts and, well, you probably won't be in Massachusetts anymore.

By the time we reach Buffalo, at the foothills of the Bighorn Mountains, Sadie has to pee. Delia's favorite pottery store is having a sale so she wants to pop in and take a look, which is how I find myself in the general store, flipping through the postcard display by the register. Nearly all of them have bison on them, which I guess makes sense—that's got to be where the town gets its name, right?

A buffalo with mist rising around him some cool morning. A buffalo backlit by the sunset. A whole herd of them. The store is having a sale: buy four, get a fifth for free, so I do. I figure I can send one to Mom and Dad, one to Austin, and the other three I can save for a shadow box.

Or to send to Becca.

I push that thought to the back of my mind. Send a postcard apologizing to Becca? *For real, Emma?* One: her parents might read it. Or worse: Bubbe. Or actually, the absolute worst: Becca just dumps it right in a trash can without reading it at all.

No, they're better off being used for a shadow box. I hand the postcards to the clerk and pay. By the time I get outside, Delia's already back at the car with a bag from the pottery shop. Sadie's leaning against the hood, squinting in the sun. "What'd you get?" she asks before sitting up front.

I slide into the back seat. "Just some postcards," I say, fanning them out.

"You really got a thing for bison, huh?"

I shrug, wondering if Delia remembers getting the bison stuffed animal for Austin when he was a baby. Does she know how much he likes them? That bison became his favorite animal? That maybe they still are?

"You know," Sadie says, "I heard that the other

week these Swedish tourists at Yellowstone took a picture right next to some bison that stopped by the side of the road. Like they're not huge wild animals that could totally gore you to death. They're lucky they just ended up on the news and not dead. All I'm saying is, I know they're your favorite animal, but don't try to pet them. They're not exactly huge stuffed animals."

No kidding, Sadie. "Wait—that really happened?" I ask.

"Sadly more often than you'd think," Delia says. She pulls back onto the road. Bye-bye, Buffalo; hello, mountains. "Actually, that reminds me. Would you girls want to take a trip out there later this summer?"

"To Yellowstone?" Sadie asks.

"Yeah," Delia says. "It's been a few years since we've been, and it'd be the first time for Emma."

"Everything out here's a first for Emma, but that doesn't mean *I've* got to trek all over the place."

Delia lets that one fly and focuses on me. "What do you think, Em?"

I can't tell her what I really think: that I don't deserve this. A vacation inside of a vacation, but without the rest of my family. It doesn't feel fair, and yet of course I want to go. To see a real live buffalo up close—well, not as close as those Swedish tourists. But to see them just roaming about, like how it used to be for them, when it was just bison and Native Americans living out here, centuries ago.

"That sounds really nice," I say, which is the truth too. "Would Chris come?"

"He's got some longer off stretches later this summer, so hopefully. We'll have to look into lodging and all of that when we're back in town. Gets pretty busy with all the kids out of school, but I bet we can swing it."

"Oh, if it's really hard, then don't worry about it."

Delia bats away my reply. "We're going. It's settled."

Late that night I wake up to rain drumming on the roof of the tent, slow and steady. Sadie and I put the rain fly on earlier, but I reach my hands out along the edges of the tent, nervous that all this time, water's been seeping in. Maybe it's my O'Malleyness, expecting the worst since it's a camping trip. But it's dry at the edges.

Even though it's dark, I can make out the lump

next to me. Sadie's nose makes a soft whistling sound every now and then.

I don't know why I thought sharing a tent would help me connect with her. Or why I even want to, anyway, except to make sure I'm not disappointing my mom. She texted the other day, asking how Sadie is, and I said she's nice because, well, what else could I say? I already reminded her that Sadie is two years older than me. Sure, we're closer in age than me and Austin, but Sadie's not my sister, and she's not going to pretend for a few months either.

Not that I want a sister. Not that anyone could ever come close to Austin.

I'm not sure Mom and Dad thought things out too far when they took Delia up on her offer anyway. Having me out here let them check a zillion things off their list all at once. I get it, I do. But that doesn't make it easier for me, exactly. Just easier for them.

Maybe I didn't think it through either when I said yes. What exactly am I going to do here for an entire two months? Sure, I told Kennedy and Lucy I was going to be an artist, but how does that work? All my stuff is at home. All I have here is my sketchbook and, okay, five postcards. Also, even if I wanted to, I can't make shadow boxes all day long, every day. My fingers would fall off.

Or get glued together.

Or both.

It's like I'm starting from scratch in every way.

CHAPTER TWENTY

By the time we return to town late Monday night, I'm starting to think camping's not so bad after all. And not just because I managed to survive three days of it.

I couldn't admit it in front of Sadie, but it turns out it actually *is* nice to leave your smartphone behind. To be fair, aside from the occasional text from Lucy, I was only getting texts from Mom and Dad, which is pretty pathetic if I spend too long thinking about it. But by leaving my phone behind, I wasn't thinking about that. Instead I was noticing the way the light caught the dewdrops suspended in a spider's web. The soft snapping of a twig as we hiked a trail. The warmth of the sun on my shoulder when we finally reached a clearing.

I knew when we got back into town, I'd have to start figuring it out: what I was going to do with the next two months in Wyoming. But for two days I didn't have to focus on that. I just got to breathe.

Tuesday morning, I'm at the kitchen table eating a bowl of granola with almond milk when the doorbell rings. Delia's still in her sweats from her morning yoga class. She invited me to tag along, but given that in gym class I once knocked over Jesse Polito doing tree pose, I politely declined. Sure, I need to find some way to fill up this summer, but yoga is not it.

Delia gets up to answer the door.

"Emma?" she yells from the living room. "It's for you."

For . . . me?

But nobody here even knows me. Still, I clink my spoon in my cereal bowl and pad into the living room.

Sitting on the sofa is Tyler from the library. He's wearing the same white pants as when I met him—the kind I for sure would stain in less than five minutes—with a plaid purple button-down shirt.

I cross my arms over my chest, suddenly self-conscious about being in my pajamas, even though there's hardly anything to cover up. Becca might have gotten real boobs last summer, but I've still got the chest of an eight-year-old.

"Finally, you're back! I came by yesterday, but you weren't here."

"We went camping. Wait—how do you know where I live?"

"Well, you're staying with Sadie. And I had Mrs. Sadowski for fifth grade."

"Oh," I say. How small is this town, exactly?

"Well, I'll let you two be. Holler if you need anything, Em." Delia heads back into the kitchen.

"You got any plans today?" I catch it there again, that little bit of lilt to his voice that says he's from Wyoming.

I shake my head.

"Want to hang out?"

"Sure," I say. "No offense, but what is there to do around here besides the library?"

"Ouch." Tyler rubs at a spot on his chest like I've just pierced his heart.

"Actually, is there a Goodwill or a Take It or Leave It in town? Or a flea market?"

Tyler's eyes light up. "You want to go shopping?"

"Sort of," I say.

"I'm game."

I'm all ready to slip into some shoes and leave with Tyler when I remember I'm still in my pajamas. "Can I go get dressed?"

"Nope, it's a requirement. We can only go shopping if you stay in your pajamas."

I laugh. "I'll be right back."

I'm halfway down the stairs when Tyler shouts, "Does Mrs. Sadowski still have that cat she always talked about in class? Gandalf?"

"Dumbledore," I shout back up the stairs. "But watch out, he can turn on you in a second."

After changing into shorts and a tank top, I grab the two buffalo postcards I filled out for my parents and Austin. I'm pulling out the address for the rehab center when the piece of paper about the art competition falls out of my backpack. There aren't that many rules for this one. All that's included is the deadline, information about how to submit the art, size constraints, and this: "The principles of true art is not to portray, but to evoke."

Beneath the quote is the name Jerzy Kosinski. I don't know who that is. An artist? Some person who runs the contest?

"Ow! You vicious beast! You're no Dumbledore. You're Draco Malfoy. You're Lord Voldemort himself. Hey, Em, this cat's some kind of Dementor."

"Don't provoke him, then!" I shout back.

"I was just trying to pet him."

Across the way, the door opens. Sadie stands in the frame, rubbing sleep out of her eyes. "Where are you headed this early in the morning?"

"To Goodwill. With Tyler."

"Look at you, making friends already." She nods like she's impressed, then heads down the hall toward the bathroom.

I toss my wallet and buffalo book in my backpack, surprised by how my mouth keeps breaking into a smile. It feels good hearing that word. Could I really have a friend here already?

"Can we stop by the post office on the way?" I ask as I hop onto Sadie's old bike outside. Tyler's is looking a little rough—the front fender is banged up and he could use a bit more air in the tires, plus it looks too small for him.

"You got some mail to send your *boyfriend*?" Tyler teases.

I laugh. "No." If some boy from back home teased me like that, I'd probably blush or feel all awkward, but I don't with Tyler. He acts like we've known each other for years even though we've barely spent half an hour together. He's not so closed off like people are back home. His heart feels a little more open.

Maybe it's a Wyoming thing. Delia seems that way too.

"It's for my brother," I say, and then I wonder if that sounds weird. Like, wouldn't it also be for my parents? Wouldn't I just say my *family*?

But Tyler doesn't ask that question. "Older or younger?"

"Older."

"I always wanted an older brother," Tyler says, almost wistfully. "What's he like?"

"He's . . ." The answer used to come so easily. Athletic. Popular. Ridiculous—well, if you spent enough time around him. But now I don't even know where to start. I can't tell him the truth. Tyler barely knows me. Plus, what do people think about family members of addicts, anyway? That they should've known? Should've been able to do something to stop it?

Sometimes I think that deep down, part of me was in denial. I couldn't believe something that bad could be happening with *my* brother.

"I know. It's pretty impossible to describe someone you know that well. Maybe someday I'll get to meet him. Do you guys FaceTime?"

We would if he weren't in rehab. But then again, if he weren't in rehab, I wouldn't be here in the first placc. Just as I'm about to say something vague back, I notice an animal in the grassy field off to the side of the bike path. With the body of a deer and long, twisty horns, it looks like something out of a safari exhibit at the zoo. "What the heck is that?"

"The antelope? They're basically like squirrels," Tyler says.

"Like squirrels? Have you seen a squirrel? That thing's huge and—"

"Not *technically* like a squirrel. Just as in how many

there are around here. How have you not seen any antelope yet?"

I shrug, relieved that the antelope has gotten us off the topic of my brother.

At the post office, I hop off my bike, careful to keep my hand over the address on the postcard. I don't want anyone—not Tyler, not even a stranger—to see where it's going.

After I slide the postcard in the blue box, I can't help but think about the other three in my bag. Becca has no idea I'm in Wyoming. Unless my mom decided to tell hers. What's my mom even saying to people, anyway? Like when she runs into someone we know at the grocery store? When people back home ask how the kids are, can she answer like she used to, not skipping a beat, "Oh, they're great"? Even though one of us is in Wyoming and the other in rehab?

As weird as it is for me here, it's got to be weirder back home for Mom and Dad.

When we get to Goodwill, the cool air-conditioning hits me and it's like diving into a pool on a hot summer day. "Ahhh," I say, throwing my hands up in the air. I can't help myself. I don't know how Tyler wears pants in the summer here.

"So, what are you looking for?" Tyler asks.

"I don't know." It's the truth. It's also why most people back home hate to shop with me. I head to the back of the store, where I always start, to the shelves of odds and ends, housewares, et cetera, where you never know exactly what you'll find. I pick up a tarnished spoon, holding it up to the light.

"Mrs. Sadowski's silverware not good enough for you? Though, I'll be honest, that one looks like it's seen better days."

"Exactly," I say. "Sorry. I'm not doing a good job explaining myself. It's for my art."

"Your *art*." Tyler looks impressed. And he's doing that repeating-me thing, which I actually find kind of hilarious when it's him, even if someone else doing it would drive me up the wall.

"I make these boxes. Shadow boxes. I find stuff that catches my eye—that could tell a story, I guess. Stuff that you don't think would go together, but somehow it does."

"Like this old dish and a . . ." Tyler scans for

something super random. "Toilet plunger?"

"Ew. But yeah. Except not a toilet plunger. But you get the idea."

Tyler puts down the toilet plunger, his face totally giving away his regret. "That's cool, Em."

I raise an eyebrow. "You don't think it's weird?"

"Well, it's different, I guess. But weird? I think everything's a little weird if you spend too much time thinking about it. It's your thing and it makes you happy. So what if it's weird?"

It's something about the way he says it, or maybe it's that he says it at all. That he's okay with weirdness—mine, anyone's—but I can't stop myself from blushing a little. I turn toward the shelf, not wanting him to notice, and that's when I see it.

An astronaut Barbie. The exact same kind Becca got for her eighth birthday. She hated Barbies—we both did—and so after her party, where she did a medium-good job of pretending she liked the gift, we did what any nerdy third grader would do.

We launched her. Not into space, just over Becca's house. With her birthday money, Becca went out and bought the gift she actually wanted, a model rocket kit, and while she worked on that, I got Barbie ready for her maiden—okay, only—voyage. I gave her a tattoo sleeve—stars, obviously—and a good haircut. (Who's got time to wash that much hair in space?)

Unfortunately, we didn't get the launch angle exactly right, and Barbie didn't so much go *over* Becca's roof as get caught on one of the back gables. Her dad kept saying he'd call someone to come get her down, but he clearly wasn't prioritizing it, because by the time someone came with a tall enough ladder, she'd vanished.

Some bird must've flown off with her. That was Becca's theory, anyway.

I wasn't so sure. I liked to think Barbie didn't give up on that first try, when things didn't go quite right, and that she launched herself into the outer reaches of the atmosphere one cool winter night.

There's no price tag on the Barbie, but there's a sign on the top of the shelf saying everything in this aisle is two dollars. I grab a basket from the end of the aisle and add her to it, and that's when it hits me: how I can win Becca back.

Not with a postcard. Not with something I write.

I mean, who am I kidding? I've never been much of a writer.

I need to show her that I remember what our friendship means. And what better way to do that than with a shadow box? I've got almost two months to make it. Two months to fill it with everything that can remind Becca of how we used to be.

And then when I go home at the end of the summer, I can give it to her myself. Maybe we need this time, Becca and me, to see what we're missing. What we lost by drifting apart this year. And then we can go back.

Just like rehab is helping Austin go back to how he used to be, this box will help me and Becca.

Tyler and I scan the shelves of Goodwill. I don't tell him what I'm making yet, or why. Not that everything that goes in my basket is just for Becca's box. Sometimes things just catch my eye—I save them for later, not knowing why I'll need them, only sure that they have some purpose. Plus I have two months here. Plenty of time to make several shadow boxes.

Eventually our stomachs are growling and I've collected more random stuff than will fit in my backpack. At the register, the elderly lady ringing us up marvels at the sheer range of our findings. Old magazines, the astronaut Barbie, the tarnished spoon, random old postcards, some beaded necklaces, marbles, and a couple of toy cars like the ones Austin had as a little kid. "So, who's your new friend, Tyler?"

"Emma," he says proudly. "She's here from Baaahston." He turns to me. "Better?"

"B-plus."

Tyler seems pleased with himself.

"Boston, huh?" She shows me my total. All this stuff for fifteen dollars and some change! "Don't see too many folks from your neck of the woods out here."

I hand her a twenty. "My mom came out here when she was in college," I say. "She wanted me to have an adventure this summer." So far, Tyler hasn't asked any more questions about this reasoning. Maybe in his head, it's something people back in Boston do all the time. Send their kids off to remote locations for the heck of it.

"Well, I'm sure our friend Tyler can make that happen." I help her put what doesn't fit in my backpack into two plastic bags. "Have a good one, you two," she calls after us. The bell by the door jingles while Tyler holds it open for me.

"You have a lot of old-lady friends?" I ask on the way out, teasing Tyler.

"Actually, yeah." His voice suddenly sounds more serious. "She's good friends with my grandma," he says. "I live with my grandparents."

"Oh," I say as I try to figure out how to attach these bags to my bike so they won't whack me the whole way home. "That's . . ." But I don't know how to finish the sentence. I can't say *I'm sorry*, even though that's what almost comes out. For all I know, he prefers it this way. Still, part of me wants to ask Tyler why he doesn't live with his parents. But then the other part thinks of how kind he was earlier not to pry about my brother. "Can I meet them sometime?"

"They work during the day. Grams at the grocery store, and Gramps at the mines."

"Chris—Mr. Sadowski—he works there too," I say, though inside, I'm wondering if both of Tyler's parents are dead. How awful. How unfair.

Tyler takes one look at what I've done to my bike and laughs. "Okay, clearly you have never had to carry anything on a bike before."

"True."

He unwinds the plastic bags from the handles and secures them to the sides. "Much better. So, where to next?"

"Back to Delia's?"

"To Delia's!" He pumps his fist. "Okay, sorry, it's really weird calling her anything other than Mrs. Sadowski when she used to be my teacher. How about this: Back to your place?"

"Back to my place." Now I'm the one who feels weird, thinking of Delia's house as *my* place.

By the time we're back at Delia's, the sky has clouded over, which finally makes the temperature somewhat bearable. We bring my bags of Goodwill treasures downstairs. Sadie and Delia are nowhere to be found. There's a note on the kitchen table: *Went out for a bit. Be back around 2 p.m. Help yourselves to anything for lunch. XO, D.*

I grab a jar of salsa and a container of guacamole from the fridge, along with a new bag of tortilla chips.

Tyler peeks out the window. "Storm's coming in."

"It's just cloudy," I say.

"We don't do cloudy in the summer. It's either a storm or it's hot as heck. Do you want to go up on the roof and watch?"

"Up on *the roof*?" Now I'm doing the repeating thing.

Turns out it's not as dangerous as I would've thought. For one, Delia's house isn't nearly as tall as mine or Becca's. And two, you can reach the roof pretty easily by climbing the back deck.

The shingles are still hot from the midday sun, but I lay a blanket across them like Tyler suggests. Just as I'm sitting down, my phone buzzes with a text from my mom. Having fun?

Tyler sees it too, and as I start typing a response, he says, "You better tell her I'm fun!"

"Telling her I had the worst day ever. With this awful boy Tyler who won't leave me alone."

Tyler sticks out his tongue at me. I do it back. I think I made a new friend today. Having lots of fun. Miss you.

For a second I feel the worst kind of guilt. Because it's true, I am having fun today. When's the last time someone stopped by my house three days in a row just to see if I could hang out? Never. Not even Becca. I don't deserve Tyler. I'm not sure I deserve any of this.

I crack open the salsa and dip in a chip. And then all I can think about is the spiciness hitting my tongue and that we're up on the roof with spicy salsa and I completely forgot drinks.

Mom writes back, So happy to hear this. Miss you lots.

Suddenly it occurs to me that even though Tyler won't be able to meet Austin via FaceTime, I do have photos of him on my phone. "Do you want to see a picture of my brother?"

"Yeah, sure."

I flip all the way back to last August. My parents had rented a house on the Cape for two weeks. The Grossmans came down for the weekend in the middle. I skip past the pictures of me and Becca and our epic sandcastle until I find one of Dad and Austin. Dad's wearing his Celtics shirt. Austin's flexing like a goof, and he's got his Patriots hat on backward. My fingers leave a salty smear on my phone as I pass it off to Tyler. "That's Austin."

"He kind of looks like a young Christopher. You know, from *Gilmore Girls*?"

I shake my head—I've never seen *Gilmore Girls*, though I know Kennedy watched some of it with her moms.

"He's cute in that preppy way. I mean, not that I—he's too old for me. Ugh. Now I seem like a weirdo, creeping on your brother." He shoves a few chips in his mouth. "Okay, but actually, he is. He's really cute. I mean, not that you're—ugh. I should not even be allowed to talk anymore. Shut up, Tyler. Shut up."

"It's fine," I say. "You're not the first person who's ever said that." I was right earlier, in the library. But it doesn't seem like Tyler wants to make a fuss over it now, so I don't say anything about it.

"I don't even know why you want to hang out with me. Your family is *beautiful.* You get to travel all over the country like it's no big deal. Twenty dollars is *nothing* to you. I haven't even been on a plane yet! The farthest I've been is South Dakota. And not even Sioux Falls, just Rapid City."

I can't let him go even one second longer thinking that I'm on some higher tier than him, when really, I'm like a basement dweller on the good-human scale. "Tyler, stop."

He's halfway through a chip when I say it, so he just chews for a second while I try to figure out what to say next. So many confessions compete for the chance to come out. *Actually, aside from you, I have no friends right now. Like, literally zero. I sold out my old best friend. I missed every sign of my brother's addiction. And that adventure? My parents sent me away for the entire summer to stay with people I barely know. They have no clue who I really am or all of what went down this year. And if they knew the truth?*

"He's in rehab—Austin, I mean." There it is. It's out. I can almost feel something inside me lift, like my whole body is lighter from having said it out loud.

Licking tortilla chip dust off my fingers, I stare out into the distance. That's what we came up here to do, right? Watch the storm roll in.

Far off to the west, dark clouds have gathered. The patch of sky below them is the darkest blue-gray. Before coming here, I'd never seen a rainstorm that way. How the rain filled the sky, from the clouds all the way down to the earth.

It's not just an expression. You can literally see it coming from miles away.

The only way you could miss it is if you were looking the other way entirely.

And I was. I had been, back at home. I'd been so busy falling in with Kennedy and Lucy that I hadn't realized what was going on with my own brother.

CHAPTER TWENTY-ONE

Before Tyler has a chance to reply, Delia's car pulls into the driveway. Is she going to be mad we're up on the roof? Mom and Dad would be, but Delia's different.

Sadie steps out first, scrunching her nose as she stares up at us. "What the heck are you doing on the roof?"

Tyler answers first. "Watching the storm. You want to join us?"

"I think I'll pass, but you two have fun up there."

Delia squints at us. "Enjoying the change in perspective?"

"You bet, Mrs. Sadowski."

When she follows Sadie inside, Tyler turns to me. "I'm sorry about your brother. Is that why you came here? To get away?"

I can't tell him the truth: how it is and it isn't. How getting away also makes things easier for me. How two weeks from now I was supposed to start that camp in Providence, with my two new best friends who now aren't.

If I told him the whole truth, he wouldn't want to hang out with me. And then I'd have no one again. So instead I say, "Yeah," and leave it at that.

Eventually the storm draws so close that we have no choice but to come down off the roof and head inside. I'm still stuffed from the chips and salsa, but Tyler's hungry, so we make PB&J sandwiches and take them down to the den.

There's a huge table that Delia uses for quilting, but right now it's empty, so we take it over, dumping out all the stuff from Goodwill. It's just a start. But spreading it out helps me imagine things in new combinations. See what's missing and what could be.

I flip open one of the magazines and skim through the pictures, cutting pages out now and then when something catches my eye. A sunset. A cool shot of a bird slicing over the water. The most vivid blue butterflies I've ever seen. None of them are quite right for my Becca box, but maybe they'll work for another one. Maybe something will come together that's perfect for the art contest.

Tyler thumps the table with a stack of books from his backpack and starts reading the first one. It's thick—at least twice as long as my buffalo book. Hey, maybe that's what another shadow box could be about. Bison! I pop over to my room for the buffalo book.

Soon I'm jotting down notes about bison in my sketchbook, not knowing where it'll take me, but jazzed about the possibilities. Bison may look enormous, but it turns out those guys can run. Up to thirty-five miles per hour in short bursts. Way, way faster than my mom. Maybe even faster than Austin when he used to sprint.

Not only can they move fast, but they can turn quickly while running, like if they need to dodge something. They've got excellent hearing and a keen sense of smell, but they can't see very well for a distance. Like Dumbledore, their body language gives off signs about their mood. A relaxed tail means they're chill. A stiff horizontal tail means they're excited. And a tail pointing straight up means *watch out*. That buffalo is angry and might charge you.

I write it all down, not just because it could help with a shadow box, but so I'll remember in case we make it out to Yellowstone later this summer.

"I give up," Tyler says, setting that thick book down on the table. "There are way too many characters to keep track."

"What's the book?" He holds it up to show me. *Anna Karenina* by Leo Tolstoy. "Isn't that an adult book?"

"Yeah. And it's Russian, so everyone's name has a bajillion syllables. But I like how it starts." He flips it open to read aloud. "'All happy families are alike; each unhappy family is unhappy in its own way.' I know that Tolstoy guy is dead and lived in Russia like a hundred years ago or something, but he totally gets it."

My mind flashes to a few hours ago on the roof—what I told Tyler about Austin. Does he think my family is unhappy?

Are we?

This feels like my chance to ask about why he doesn't live with his parents. "Your mom and dad . . ." I start to say, but I don't know how to finish. I can't say, *are they dead?* "Do you . . . still see them?"

Tyler fiddles with the cover of the book like he's trying to figure out how much to say.

"I don't even know who my dad is," he says. "And my mom . . . well, I could see her. I'm not going to, but I could." His eyes flash up at me before returning to focus on his book. He clears his throat. "You're probably going to find out anyway, so I might as well tell you."

"You don't have to," I say, though I don't know what he's talking about. Something Delia would know? Sadie?

"Today was so nice. Too nice." He stands up, gathering his stuff together. "I guess I should've known it would end."

"Tyler, stop. What are you talking about?"

He zips his backpack up quickly and heads for the door.

"Tyler, wait!" The chair falls to the floor behind me as I jump up from where I've been sitting. He's surprisingly fast, up the stairs and out the front door before I catch up with him.

"Don't leave," I say, breathless. *You're my only friend here.* "I get it. I do. You don't have to say anything you don't want to. Not with me."

"No," he says, shaking his head at me. "You don't get it. You have no idea what it's like being known as the kid whose mom has a drug problem that landed her in prison. Having the whole thing play out in the news so everyone at the school knows. *Everyone.*"

Prison? A drug problem?

"Tyler, it's okay. I don't care."

"Look, you say that and I know you think you mean it and that it helps . . . but it doesn't. I can already see you trying to figure the rest out. You do, you want to know. Everyone wants to know. That's all you see now when you look at me."

I hate that he's a little bit right, but I know deep down he's also wrong. There have to be plenty of people who see Tyler for who he is and not just whatever happened with his mom. "Don't go. Please, Ty. I won't say that I know what it's like because I don't, but—look, I don't need to know any more. Whatever you want to talk about or don't, that's fine. Our unhappy families are different. You were right. Tolstoy was right. I guess

Russians do know something besides how to rig the Olympics."

Tyler cracks a smile there. If there's one thing I learned from Kennedy, it's that Russian figure-skating judges are not to be trusted.

"So can you come back inside?" I say. "We could watch something. *Gilmore Girls*?"

He takes a few steps toward me. "You've really never seen it?"

"Not even one episode. You can introduce me to it."

"Where you lead, I will follow."

"Huh?"

"You'll understand in a few minutes. You're going to love it, Em. You're a good friend, you know?"

At some point I'll have to tell him what really happened back home. I can't let this feeling keep gnawing away at me. But for right now I just need to hear it. Like if I hear it enough, maybe it can be true again.

CHAPTER TWENTY-TWO

For the next few weeks, like clockwork, Tyler arrives at Delia's house every weekday morning while I'm eating my breakfast. Some days we have a plan for what we're going to do—like check out Goodwill to see if anything new and weird came in, or go to the library for a teen program (okay, mostly for the free pizza and so Tyler can get more books), or hang out at the town pool so we can spy on (I mean, maybe see) this boy Tyler has a crush on.

On the days when it's too hot to bike anywhere, we crank up the AC in Delia's basement and slowly devour a bag of Oreos while working on an art project and reading and binge-watching *Gilmore Girls.*

We both think Rory has the worst taste in guys and that Lane's boyfriend Dave Rygalski is clearly the best boyfriend on the show. He read the whole entire Bible for her! Now, that's commitment. (Tyler skipped ahead to show me that episode—we're only on season two right now.)

I don't ask Tyler more about his mom, and he doesn't offer up any details, and that's okay. Really.

On my third Saturday in Wyoming, I'm down in the basement sketching possible interiors for my Becca box when Delia sets a small white envelope on the table beside me. "Something came for you in the mail today."

There's no return address on the envelope, and for a second my heart starts palpitating like crazy. Could it be from Becca? But then I notice it's postmarked Hyannis, Massachusetts. It's from Austin!

I open it carefully, as if what's inside is somehow delicate. A single lined sheet of paper, folded into thirds.

Hey Emma,

Thanks for sending me that postcard. I don't really get much mail here. You can tell not a lot happens when people get all jazzed about mail. Just like you! You always got a little too excited about the mail.

Anyway. Sounds like you're having fun in Wyoming, so that's cool. And it's nice to know they're taking you on trips with them. Camping? For real? Aren't you still afraid of the dark and moths? Remember that one time we went camping and you were too afraid to get up and pee in the night and you wet the bed—er, sleeping bag—and Mom thought that human pee actually lured bears so she made us throw out the sleeping bag and you had to share mine?

Yeah. That's why we O'Malleys don't do camping. Haha.

Still, Wyoming sounds cool. Especially the buffalo. I know you said you can't pet them or you might get gored, but, I don't know, seems like kind of an exciting way to go.

I'm kidding. Don't get gored by a buffalo, Emma.

Take lots of pictures so you can show me all your adventures. I won't be here that much longer. Really. I found out how much Mom and Dad are paying for this place and I almost died. So this might be your last vacation for a while.

All kidding aside, you asked how I'm doing. I'm doing good, Emma. Ugh. Well! I'm doing well. I want to stay clean. I really do. And I know a lot more now than I did before. I'm never touching that stuff again, I swear.

I'm sorry, Em. I'm so sorry about everything.

Say hi to the buffalo for me.

Love,

Austin

I must read it five times in a row before I finally set it down for a second. Tears well in my eyes. No one's down here with me—Delia went upstairs right after dropping it off, almost like she knew I'd need a moment alone with it. But for some reason, I can't let myself cry. I have to be strong, for Austin. I have to be strong, like Austin.

He doesn't really say much about himself in the letter. But he says he's doing well. Of course he is. He's Austin. The old Austin knew all about working hard. It was what he did—in school, at practice, on the football field. He knows how to put in the work.

He's going to beat this. I know it. He's got only two more weeks there, and then he'll come home. He's going to show everyone—Mom, Dad, and everyone else—that he's back to normal.

I'm never touching that stuff again, I swear.

It's a promise. And I believe him.

Late Sunday morning, I'm on the front porch reading my buffalo book when an unfamiliar beige sedan pulls into our driveway and out comes Tyler, making a beeline for me.

"What are you doing here?" I ask. "You know it's Sunday, right?"

"You said you wanted to know when there's a yard sale, and Grams's church is having a big one today and I didn't know until we went to church and saw it and I don't have your cell number so I thought—"

"Oh my gosh, Tyler. It's okay." I laugh. "I'm just

surprised, is all. Does this mean I get to finally meet your Grams?"

Tyler nods, and I head inside to let Delia know where I'm going. I don't know why it makes me nervous a little, the idea of meeting Tyler's grandmother. Maybe it's that I still don't know more about Tyler's mom. Two weeks of hanging out every weekday and it's the one subject he doesn't talk about.

I get it, though. I've been open with him about my family and Austin but real quiet about Becca and Kennedy.

Tyler opens the car door for me, all gentlemanlike, which makes me giggle, and then I slide in. The car smells like vanilla. His grandmother's hair is shoulder-length and gray, and she reaches a hand back for me to squeeze. She's younger than I imagined, definitely younger than my grandparents. "So nice to finally meet you, Emma. Tyler's been running my ear off about you these past couple weeks."

"It's nice to meet you, too."

"Tyler tells me you're from Massachusetts, huh? I've never been out east myself, but I hear it's lovely."

"Her town's like Stars Hollow," Tyler says.

"Thank goodness he's got someone else to watch that darn show with." His grandmother laughs, tapping on the steering wheel for emphasis. "Those Gilmores talk too fast. I couldn't stand one more minute of them."

Tyler rolls his eyes, snickering a little. "Grams has a few opinions."

"A few, eh? Well, I'm just glad Tyler's found himself a friend for the summer. Lord knows it hasn't been an easy year for him. He's a good kid, though, and he deserves it. It's just too bad you're not sticking around longer."

"I'll be here through most of August," I say. "We've still got a lot of time."

"I know, I know."

"Maybe sometime Tyler can come out and visit me."

"Fly? All the way out to Massachusetts?" Grams flips her sunglasses up and eyes me in the rearview mirror.

"Maybe next summer. Or at Christmas? We're stuck in Boston for the holidays anyway because of my mom's store. Might as well make the most of it."

"Well, I don't know about that," Grams says.

Something changes in her voice, and I can't figure out why. Does she not want Tyler to travel for some reason? Can't she see that he's just itching to get out of this town?

I glance over at Tyler, but he's just looking down at his lap. I've clearly overstepped some kind of boundary.

Thankfully, up ahead I can see the massive yard sale in the parking lot of the Presbyterian church. Table after table covered in all kinds of stuff, blankets spread out on the grass. But that *I'm in heaven* feeling that usually comes over me when I get to shop for shadow boxes is tamped down by the mood in the car.

Grams heads for one of her friends running the refreshments booth while Tyler and I start wandering the sale. Once she's out of earshot, I ask him, "Everything all right?"

"Yeah," Tyler says. But it's not the 150 percent enthusiastic "yeah" I'm used to getting.

I know I said I wouldn't pry, but I don't think this is about his mom, so I figure it's okay to give it a shot. "It's just, a minute ago, in the car with your Grams, it felt like—"

"She can't afford to fly me to Massachusetts, Em. But she's too proud to say it."

My face goes hot, and I feel like an idiot. "I'm sure my parents could pay. My parents always have frequent-flier miles they don't use and—"

"Em, stop. I'm not some charity case, all right? Look, I don't want to talk about it anymore."

"Okay," I say. It's the first moment we've had like this in two weeks, and I hate how it leaves me with this squirminess in my stomach. I didn't mean to hurt his feelings, but somehow I did.

I decide it's better to stay quiet than to try to say something to make things better only to have it backfire. I flip through some books, looking for any by Becca's favorite authors. The other day I thought maybe I could cut out pages from her favorite books and black out most of the words to make a poem, like we did back in fifth grade, but then I remembered the "book murderer" incident.

Book dismembering is probably at least as bad in Becca's mind, so scratch that.

I'm detangling a necklace that's gotten stuck in an old brooch when I hear Tyler excitedly calling out my name.

I hurry over to meet him at the next table. It was probably a jewelry box once, its cover made of beveled glass. Teeny-tiny squares and diamonds, angled in just right. It's beautiful: the kind of thing you inherit, not what you put out at a yard sale.

I flip it over and find a tag saying it's only five dollars.

"It's perfect," I whisper, fumbling in my pocket for some cash.

"Sorry about a minute ago," Tyler says. "I shouldn't have gotten upset."

"It's okay," I say. There's a man working this table. When I hand him the five dollars, he offers me a plastic grocery bag and a yellow sticker to slap on the box to show I've paid for it.

"It's not, though," Tyler says. "You were just being nice. I wish I could come out and visit. I want to go. You know they have an annual Stars Hollow convention in Connecticut, right?"

"Maybe you can. Look, your Grams is right: a lot has happened this year. Maybe she's afraid of you being far away. Maybe she's worried she's going to lose you, too." As I'm saying that, it hits me. Maybe that's how Mom and Dad feel right now about Austin. No one wants to send their kid away. They knew they'd have to for college, sure. Earlier this year, before everything went wrong, sometimes I'd catch them getting all wistful about it. They were so certain he'd want to go far.

And now, ahead of schedule, he is away. Just for a month, and just to Cape Cod, but still.

"I can try to warm her up to the idea," Tyler says.

Now that things seem okay with us, I pull the letter from Austin out of my back pocket. "I got this in the mail yesterday," I say, handing it to him.

"You sure you want me to read it?"

"No, I handed it to you because I don't want you to read it," I deadpan. "Yes, silly."

We pull off to the side, where there's a picnic table under a tree, and sit down next to each other. The whole time he's reading it, I keep shifting my new Becca box, creating little rainbows from the refracting light. As much as I don't want my time here in Wyoming with Tyler to end, in this moment I want to fast-forward to the end of the summer. Becca's box will be beautiful by then. No, perfect. And Austin will be home and healthy again. And we'll start the new school year and everything can just go back to the way it used to be.

Tyler hands the letter back to me. "That's . . . great, Em." I can't help noticing how his voice doesn't match the words.

"It sounds like he's doing so much better, right? I mean, he's joking in the first part. And he says how much he's learned now and how he's never going to get into that stuff again. He sounds like how he used to. I mean, not that you would know. But he does. He seems happy and hopeful. They caught it in time, you know?"

"Yeah . . ." There's that hesitation again.

"What?" I say.

"It's just—this stuff is so hard. That's what I saw with my mom. She was in and out of rehab so many times. And every time, she'd say it was the last time, but it wasn't. And so eventually I just stopped believing her. It was easier that way. Then she couldn't let me down."

"I'm sorry," I say, surprised by how easy it is to reach out and hug him.

I wish I could make his mom as strong as Austin. Wish that there were some way to give their story a happy ending. But all these unhappy families, they're different, like Tolstoy said. Some of them stay unhappy forever. And others get a second chance.

CHAPTER TWENTY-THREE

Back home I used to be the kind of person who always slept through the night, but now that I'm in Wyoming, that's no longer true.

I wake up with a start, never remembering my dream, and every time it takes me a second to figure out where I am. The streetlight outside my window back home would shine into my bedroom no matter how many times Mom or I played around with the shade. Plus it never got that dark, with the city so close by. It was comforting, that light. I know it doesn't make any sense, but as I fell asleep, it felt like someone was watching over me.

In the darkness now, as my brain remembers why I'm here, there's that little moment of panic. Austin and my parents, they're so far away. What if something happened to them? And I don't even know it yet?

My brain starts whirring with all the things that could go wrong, until I lay my eyes on the one thing that settles all the worries. My Becca box. Even though I've been working on it in the den during the day, at night I always bring it back to my room. I don't trust that Dumbledore for a second. The box sits on the desk across from my bed, and in the dark I can just barely make out the shape. A fuzzy black rectangle, but that's enough somehow. Maybe it's better that I can't see more than that, because in my head I can see the finished product.

As I close my eyes and try to fall back asleep, I imagine walking over to Becca's house. Knocking on her door. Becca opening the door and the look on her face when she sees it. Surprise and relief and something else.

She takes it in her hands and turns it over, seeing all the details I put into it. Two months' worth. I know I can't see her remembering, but I'll know she is. I'll know because she'll do that lip-biting thing she does when she reads. Except she won't be lost in some book she's imagining in her head; this time it'll be us she's imagining. Us she's remembering.

And she'll forgive me.

She can forgive me, and Austin can get better. We can all go back. I can't explain how the two are related, only that I feel it in my body, the way you know your heart is beating, your lungs are working.

This trip is like my reset button. When I finally go home at the end of the summer, everything can go back to normal.

My legs look pink, so I smear a dab of sunscreen on them. Tyler's got his face in a library book, like he always does when we're at the town pool, but when I glance up, I catch his crush Demetri getting into the snack line. Usually, Demetri is with a bunch of his friends, but right now he's alone. Entirely and totally alone.

"Ty," I whisper.

No reaction.

I poke him in the side and he yelps. "I was reading!"

"Yeah, I know, but maybe you should get a snack now." I tip my head in the direction of the snack line.

"It's not even lunchtime."

I make my eyeballs go huge. Do I have to spell it out for him? Really? I thought he was smarter than this. I clear my throat and again tip my head toward Demetri.

Ty suddenly stiffens. I know what he's about to say next because I used to be the exact same way until someone forced me out of my shell. *Someone.* I reach into my bag for my wallet. "If you don't, I will."

"You will what?"

"Have a little chat with him. I might have to tell him how I'm new in town and about my great new friend and how he's been showing me around and I might maybe say something about—"

"Don't!" Tyler pleads with me.

I pass my wallet from one hand to the other. "If you don't get in line soon, I—"

"Let me put on a shirt first." He scrambles for his button-down.

"I'm giving you ten seconds. One, two . . ."

By the time I get to ten, Tyler's heading over there, still fiddling with the last button. Okay, he did glare at me first. But he's doing it! That's the first step.

He gets into line behind Demetri and at first he

doesn't say anything. But he must know I'm watching him because he turns around to check. I flash him a thumbs-up, and his face reddens, but he's still there, so that counts for a lot, actually. And then Demetri turns around. They're talking—not a ton, but a little—and the line is moving super slow because the teens who work the snack bar are terrible at their job and probably giving free food to their friends.

Eventually, two moms and their kids get in line behind Tyler, taking away my prime viewing angle. There's no way I can go back to reading my buffalo book now.

Is this how it feels to be Kennedy? Putting things into motion. Being the instigator for once, instead of taking the back seat like I usually do. I feel strangely powerful.

Maybe it's different when the things you put into motion aren't so positive, though. Like that first night at Camp McSweeney. The feeling you're left with then, it's not butterflies in your stomach. More like a brick.

For a while I watch a group of girls gossiping right where the deep and shallow ends meet. Two of them are super close together, but the third is a little bit removed. But maybe that's just how they're standing. Maybe that's just the moment I'm catching them in.

"I could kill you." Tyler's almost at our blanket, carrying a basket of fries. But his smile doesn't exactly look deadly.

"How'd it go?" I grab a fry—crispy, hot, and salty.

"Okay," he says, a blush creeping over his face.

"You talked to him, Ty! You talked to him *and* you didn't die. What did he say? What did you say? I need a full recap."

"Okay, so first he turned around. No, wait, maybe I said, 'hi, Demetri'? I can't remember. Anyway, so then . . ."

As he gives me the recap, Tyler's smile is different than usual. Almost like he's glowing from the inside. Was that how I looked after talking to Noah? That boost of confidence from doing the thing that scared me, Kennedy gave me that. I would have never done it without her egging me on.

"Why are they always eating more food than humanly possible?" I ask Tyler, for a moment looking up from the Becca box.

"That's the magic of Gilmore."

"But *four* Thanksgiving dinners! I mean, come on."

"It's called 'wish fulfillment,' Em. What are they supposed to do? Which invite could they really turn down?"

He has a point.

I set down my tweezers and join him on the couch. My fingers are shaky from all the painstaking work I've been doing on Becca's box. It's worth it, but it definitely requires plenty of breaks.

For the past couple of days I've been skimming through books by Tamora Pierce, one of Becca's favorite authors, and writing down the best quotes about friendship. I typed them up on Delia's laptop last night and printed them out in the teeniest-tiniest font that's still readable by the bare eye. With the tweezers I've been layering them into the glass on the side of the box, after spreading a thin layer of glue. It's tiring work, but I love how it looks.

Someone thumps down the stairs, and then Sadie peeks her head in. "Mail call," she says, thunking a yellow padded envelope on the sofa.

Austin sent me a package? Of what?

"What is it?" Tyler asks.

But when I reach for it, I find that the package is covered in Kennedy's manga drawings, with my name and address lettered in Lucy's most perfect penmanship. How did they get this address? I never told them where in Wyoming I was going.

"Aren't you going to open it?" Tyler asks.

My hands tremble, except I'm not sure it's from all that careful work with the tweezers.

"I'll be right back," I say before darting out of the den, the package in my hands. I head down the hall for my bedroom and shove it in my suitcase, in the darkest corner of the closet. I'm not ready to open it and see what's inside.

I have to fix things with Becca first. Once that's done, I can figure out what to do about Kennedy and Lucy.

I suck in a deep breath and slowly let it out before returning to the den. I just want to watch Lorelai and Rory go to their last two Thanksgiving dinners and not have to think about what happened back at home. But the show is paused, and when I ask Tyler to unpause it, all he does is say my name.

"What?" I ask.

"What just happened?"

"Nothing."

"Riiiiiight." He raises an eyebrow at me.

I cross my arms and kick my feet up on the coffee table.

"Who sent you the package?"

"Just these girls I used to be friends with."

"Used to be? Dude, I wish people I *used to* be friends with would send me a package they clearly spent hours decorating."

I don't think they spent *hours* on it, but I'm not about to quibble.

"What happened with y'all?"

Part of me thinks I should just tell him. That we've spent enough time together, and he's not going to turn on me.

But then the other part feels so guilty still. Like I don't deserve his friendship at all, and if he knew the whole truth of what I did to Becca, maybe he would think he's better off without me. That I'm not the kind of person he can really trust. And would he be so wrong?

Before I've had a chance to answer him, he reaches for an Oreo. "It's okay if you don't want to talk about it. I know we promised we wouldn't make each other say things we didn't want to. And you kept up your half of the deal." He twists the Oreo apart. "But if you ever change your mind . . ."

We watch in silence as Lorelai and Rory go to Sookie and Jackson's for their deep-fried turkey.

As I grab Oreo after Oreo, stuffing myself along with the Gilmores, all I can think about is that time over at Kennedy's when we binged-watched *Haikyu!!* and how much fun we were having, the three of us. Before I brought up Becca. I still don't even get why I did it. Why is it that sometimes we feel the urge to put somebody down for a quick laugh? I know I'm not the only person who's ever done it. But I still don't understand the why of it all.

Did it really make me feel that much better? No. Not in the moment and definitely not in the long run. So why did I do it?

I try my hardest not to think about it anymore, to push all those thoughts away and watch the show.

"How come on TV shows and movies, everyone always has just one best friend?" I say, thinking out loud for a minute. "Rory has Lane. Lorelai has Sookie. How come no one ever has two best friends? Or, like, really close friends but from totally different worlds?"

"Isn't Luke kind of Lorelai's best friend too, though?" Tyler says.

"No, he's her love interest."

"But what about Paris? You haven't seen all the seasons yet, but once they're in college, Paris stops being Rory's frenemy and becomes her friend. Like, as much as Lane is because she's right there all the time."

Maybe he's right. Maybe it is possible to have more than one best friend, so long as you don't throw one of your best friends under the bus.

Tyler leaves right before dinner, even though Delia says he's more than welcome to join us any time he wants. As I'm setting the table, Delia plops down a vase of black tulips in the center, and that fast, I'm in third grade again.

Grandpa Bill died unexpectedly, a heart attack. I was having a hard time with all of it—not just losing Grandpa Bill, but death. It terrified me in a way I couldn't explain to anyone—the idea of not being there anymore. Not just Grandpa Bill, but me someday too.

Before Grandpa Bill, nobody I'd known had died. At school everyone tried to say the right things about heaven and the afterlife. How he was in a better place. Except I wasn't so sure of any of that, not the way they were. Our family didn't go to church.

But then Becca—classic Becca—brought me this picture book. *Duck, Death and the Tulip.* It looked sort of creepy, with only that long, slender duck on the cream-colored cover, but I read it anyway. Unlike everyone else who tried to comfort me, Becca hadn't expected me to be just like her. To share her same beliefs about death. She saw me for exactly who I was. She listened.

She knew me better than anyone else. When no one else could figure out the right thing to say or do, she did.

When did that change? When did she go from being the person who got me the most to someone who didn't? And can I make her again?

Can I really? Can this box be enough?

I want it to. No, I need it to. But right now I'm not so sure anymore.

After I set down water glasses at all four spots, I'm about to ask Delia if I can have one of the tulips for my Becca box, but then I remember that it won't look this way once it's dead, and so I don't.

CHAPTER TWENTY-FOUR

Today marks Austin's twenty-eighth day in rehab. Two more days, and then he gets to come home. I've been texting with Mom and Dad constantly, checking for updates, but I guess with the facility he's staying in, there really aren't many updates. According to them, everything has gone fine and Austin will be discharged on Saturday.

He's coming home. For good.

Mom says we can FaceTime once he's home. I can't wait to see him—a letter just isn't the same.

The only sort of sad thing about Austin coming home is that it means my summer in Wyoming is half-over. Only one more month with Tyler.

I'm at the kitchen sink rinsing out my cereal bowl when Sadie asks, "So where's your conjoined twin?"

"My . . . what?"

"You and Tyler hang out so much you're practically attached at the hip or the brain or . . . wherever twins are conjoined."

I place the bowl in the dishwasher and glance up at the clock. It's 9:47. He's usually here by nine thirty at the latest. "Huh."

"He didn't text you?"

"I don't even have his phone number." I haven't needed it since we spend pretty much every day together. I use my phone only to text with Mom and Dad and, okay, to play the occasional game. Delia's so impressed with me, but it hasn't been that hard.

"Maybe you should bombard him at his place. A little role reversal for once."

"I don't know where he lives." It's only as I say it out loud that it sounds weird. How well can you really know someone when you've never been to their house?

Even though I haven't been in Becca's room for more than a month, I could still draw every detail of it from memory.

"Probably on the other side of town, where all the other meth heads live." Sadie eyes me, waiting for a reaction to the last bit. "You know his mom got busted for making meth, right? It was *all over* the news. Well, our news."

Tyler's mom is in prison for *making* drugs? She was helping people—people like my brother—get addicted? No, I think. No way. Sadie's got this wrong.

"He didn't mention that, huh? No, I guess he wouldn't."

Sadie leaves the room, flicking the light switch on her way out. I run my hands under the water, turning it up so it's almost scalding. I want to wash it away, all of it. What she said can't be true. That can't be why his mom is in prison. It has to be some other student of Delia's whose mom is in prison for that. Not Tyler.

Delia invites me to go to the rec center with her, but I pass, afraid if I go, I'll miss Tyler. I hang around the house all day, not even taking the bike for a ride. Down in the den, I work on my Becca box. It doesn't feel right to watch the next episodes of *Gilmore Girls* without Tyler, even though he's seen them all before, so instead I queue up the Harry Potter movies to keep me company as I finish gluing in all the friendship quotes.

I've set it aside to dry when Sadie gets back from hanging out with friends and joins me on the sofa. "Still no Tyler?"

I shake my head. All afternoon I've been running over our conversations from yesterday. Did I say something that upset him? Is it because Austin's about to come home and his mom is still in prison? Is that it?

I don't know what it could be, but I hate the unsettled feeling I have now. I need the Ron to my Harry. The Lane to my Rory? Maybe the Sookie to my Lorelai. I think that comes closest.

By dinnertime Tyler still hasn't shown up, and I figure it's a lost cause for the day. But if he doesn't show up tomorrow, I'm asking Delia to take me to his house. Maybe he got sick? In any case, I need to make sure he's okay.

For once Chris is home in time for dinner. He's off the entire next week. We're out on the back patio, about to dig into some Thai takeout, when the doorbell rings. Delia starts to stand up, but I tell her, "I'll get it," hoping somehow it's Tyler.

"Sure you don't mind?"

"Mom, she practically lives here," Sadie says.

She's not wrong. It's funny how this place feels like a second home.

I open the door, and there he is. My conjoined twin. Except he doesn't look as put together as usual. Tyler's purple shirt is rumpled, and he's wearing a pair of Adidas shorts that don't go with the rest of his outfit. "Sorry for not coming over like regular."

"It's okay," I say. I hate that the first thought running through my head right now is the real reason his mom's in prison. Even more, I hate that Tyler was right. I can't forget it. But there's so much more to Tyler than his mom.

"When I was about to head over this morning, my mom called."

"Did you talk to her?"

When Tyler nods, I detect the faintest traces of puffiness around his eyes. "I haven't in a while though. I just let Grams talk to her. Like if I don't talk to her, it's not real."

I get that. Maybe Mom and Dad thought sending me to Wyoming would make it easier for me not to think about Austin, but that's not true. It's impossible to forget when you're two thousand miles away and he's the reason.

"Emma?" Delia calls out from the patio. "Everything okay?"

"Do you want to stay for dinner? We just got Thai."

Tyler points at himself and raises his eyebrows. "You're eating me for dinner?"

I stroke my chin. "I'm still trying to decide which version will be the tastiest. Ty green curry? Pad Ty? Come on," I say, reaching out my hand.

His palm is sweaty from the bike ride over, but he holds on to me tight.

In the middle of dinner Chris makes an announcement. Something came up with one of his coworkers and now they need someone to take over their Yellowstone reservations. Would we be ready to go on such short notice—leaving this Saturday, two days from now?

"This is perfect!" Delia grins. "What do you think, girls?"

"Sounds good to me," I say, though I wish we could take Tyler with us. (Are we really that conjoined?)

Sadie's arms are crossed as she stares down at her dinner plate.

"Sades?" Delia asks.

"I had plans for this weekend."

"I know it's last-minute," Chris says, "but everything's booked solid for later this summer."

"Can't I just stay home? I've already been to Yellowstone a billion times." Sadie spears a piece of tofu and swipes it through the massaman curry sauce.

"But summer school is done now. I thought you'd be excited for a chance to skip out of town. Besides, this is a chance for us to get away as a family—"

Sadie shifts back in her seat, her fork clinking on the plate. "Last I checked, *she's* not in our family."

Chris folds up his napkin. "Now, that's enough."

"Seriously? You expect me to rearrange my whole summer for this girl I haven't seen since I was a toddler and it's not fair. It's not my fault her brother got sent to rehab and her parents didn't know what to do with her."

"Sadie." The spot between Delia's eyebrows scrunches together, and this time her voice is sharp—stern, even.

I'm stuck. Glued to this chair in Wyoming, where I don't belong in the first place. The thing is, I tried. I tried to take one for the team. I tried to fit in with this family. But Sadie's right. They're not my family. This isn't my home. And I don't belong here.

All I want is to disappear, to beam myself back to Massachusetts and somehow take Tyler with me.

As Delia and Chris lay into Sadie, I slip away. I'm padding down the carpeted stairs, heading for my room, when Tyler calls after me, "Emma, wait."

Halfway down the stairs, I stop and sit, the tears spilling over, until Tyler's warm body is next to me. There's this long scar on his knee I don't remember from before. When I look up from my hands, it's all that I see. A reminder that I don't know him and he doesn't know me. Not as much as we think we do.

"She's a jerk," he says.

"She's right."

"She just said that 'cause she's mad she can't do what she wants. She doesn't mean it."

At my house, Mom and Dad would never have let me run off like this. One of them would've stayed with Austin and the other would've come after me. Usually

Dad for me, Mom for Austin. But I guess that's what they're used to. Two parents, two kids. You do the math.

But Delia and Chris, they don't know how to do it. The math is still new. Never mind that Sadie's right. I'm not their kid. I'm just a guest.

"They did it, though. My mom and dad, they *did* send me away. I didn't have a say in any of it." I swipe beneath my runny nose with my hand. "And the worst part is I was kind of glad to leave. Not them and my brother—everything else."

"It's stressful."

"No, not that." I shake my head. "It's—" I squeeze my eyes shut, as if that will change anything. But even in the darkness, outside it's still Delia and Chris and Sadie, yelling at each other. And inside I'm still me. You can travel two thousand miles, but you can't get away from yourself.

I open my eyes. What do I really have to lose at this point? "I ruined my best friend's life."

Tyler stares back at me blankly. "Back home?"

"Yeah," I say. And bit by bit it falls out. How much I liked hanging out with Kennedy and Lucy. How I'd finally found friends that "got" me. And then how it all came crashing down. Because those friends who got me, they didn't get something else. That even if Becca wasn't my best friend anymore, she was still my friend. I would never, ever want to sell her out like that. I never meant to.

But by saying what I did to Kennedy and Lucy, I did. I'd planted the seed. And in the spring, it finally grew.

"The whole school knows. The *whole* school, Tyler."

"I know what that's like." He runs his hands over his knees. Outside it's gotten quiet.

"What do you mean?"

"Try going from being known as the only gay kid who's out in the sixth grade to suddenly being the gay kid whose mom got sent to prison for making meth."

Ouch. Suddenly, Becca being known as the sixth grader who still has a kitty blanket doesn't sound so terrible. "That must be hard."

"Well, it wasn't easy." He eyes me. "You didn't even flinch when I said it. Did someone tell you?"

I can't look Tyler in the eye.

"Sadie?"

"Only this morning."

Tyler takes a deep breath. "I thought if I told you, you wouldn't want to hang out with me anymore. That you'd be mad."

"At you?" He shrugs, and I shake my head. "You're not her."

"I know." Tyler shifts in the stairway. "On the phone today, she said she wanted me to come visit her. Her fortieth birthday's coming up soon."

"What did you say?"

"I told her I'd think about it." He rests his head in his hands. "I don't know, Em. I don't know if I'm ready. Or what she'll think if I come. I don't want her to think it's okay, that I've forgiven her already, because I haven't. Do you know how long she's locked up for?"

Sadie didn't tell me, so I shake my head.

"Fifteen years."

I don't mean to gasp, but one sneaks out. That's more years than I've been alive. So many I actually can't imagine how long that would feel like.

"I mean, maybe if she's on her best behavior she can get out a little early on parole, but by the time she's out and free, I'll be a grown-up." His voice breaks on that last word. "God, how could she be so selfish?" Tyler's hands are balled up into fists, and for a second I worry he's going to punch a wall or something.

"I don't know. I'm sorry."

"Me too." He slowly uncurls his fingers. "I guess . . . I feel bad because I don't think anyone else is visiting her besides Grams and Gramps, but I don't really want to go yet. I'm not ready. I don't know when I'll ever be ready."

"Emma? Tyler?" Delia comes to a stop at the top of the stairwell. "I'm so sorry, you two. I really—I'm ashamed of how we behaved tonight. All of us. You deserve better. I know the food's gotten cold, but if you want, I'd love to take you out for some ice cream. What do you say?"

Tyler and I look at each other, and I can tell he wants to take her up on the offer.

"Sure," I tell Delia.

Tyler and I take the back seat in Delia's car. She's quieter, not the normal chatty Delia. Is she embarrassed Tyler was there for all of that? One of her former students suddenly seeing her as a real person?

Finally she breaks the silence. "Now, I forget, Tyler, are you an only child or do you have siblings?"

"Just me," he says. "Why mess with perfection?"

Oh, Tyler.

I wish he could come with us to Yellowstone, but even if Delia said he could, I doubt that his grandmother would be okay with it. When I get back, we'll have only three weeks left together. Just thinking about that makes my heart twinge.

I know I need to go home, but every now and then there are these moments when I just want to stay.

CHAPTER TWENTY-FIVE

By Friday evening we're all packed up for the trip. Chris says we have to leave at the crack of dawn, which I have to say seems pretty unlikely given how late Sadie's been sleeping in since summer school ended, but I let him believe that for now. Earlier, Sadie apologized for the things she said last night, and I forgave her.

The thing is, she isn't entirely wrong. What she said was true; it just wasn't nice. Sort of like what I said about Becca's kitty blanket.

At least Sadie didn't wait so long to make things right.

As the sun sets, I'm on the living room sofa trying to finish my buffalo book. I was making good progress on it before I got derailed with all the reading for the Becca box. Of course her favorite books have to be five-hundred-page fantasy novels and not something I could read faster, like comic books or graphic novels.

Now that I'm down to the last thirty pages and about to leave for Yellowstone, I'm even more excited to see bison in person again. Delia mapped out all the spots they frequent so we can maximize our chances of seeing them. Sadie's now referring to the trip as BisonFest, which I think is a sign that even though she's bummed to be away from her friends for a week, she's not *that* bummed.

Dumbledore is licking my big toe—that cat, man—when my phone starts buzzing. "Mom?"

"Emma! So glad we're able to catch you before you left! I wasn't sure how cell reception would be in the park."

"Hey, E!" Dad chimes in.

Ever since I've been in Wyoming, they've called this way. It's kind of dorky, imagining them hovering over the same cell phone just to talk to me, but also kind of sweet.

"Is everything okay?"

"Yeah, hon. Everything's great," Mom says. "We just got off the phone with the supervisor, and everything's a go with your brother tomorrow."

"He's coming home!" I bolt up on the sofa, my sudden movement sending Dumbledore scampering off.

"He's coming home," Dad repeats. Only his voice doesn't sound as excited as mine. He sounds almost worried, which is strange because out of the two of them, Mom's usually the bigger worrier.

"He's made really good progress over the past thirty days," Mom says. "He'll still be attending group meetings every day and seeing his counselor twice a week—at least to start."

"Did you get to talk to him?"

"Not yet, nope," Mom says. "But we've been sending him letters. There's this local support group I started going to, up on the North Shore. It's been really good to meet other folks who've gone through this. It'll be nice to have their support when Austin's back."

"That's great, Mom. Have you . . . have you told anyone in town yet?"

Dad clears his throat. "About that, Emma."

"Actually—" Mom butts in.

"Let me say my piece," Dad says, "and then you can say yours."

My heart starts palpitating a little. My parents never used to fight, but it's hard to ignore how they sound right now. Like they're not on the same page at all.

"Sorry, Emma," Mom says. For a moment there's only silence, and I can't tell if they've muted the phone for a second or if they're just mouthing at each other.

"Your mom and I have had a hard time deciding the best way to come forward about Austin," Dad finally says.

"So it's still a secret?"

"Not exactly," Mom says. "Once Austin is home, it'll be easier to suss this all out, but for the time being, we've just been keeping things close to the vest. With Dad being in the public eye so much, it's . . . it's just tricky, is all."

"Do any of your friends know?"

"Only Delia," Mom says.

My heart breaks, thinking about how for the past four weeks, Mom's gone to her shop and not been able to tell anyone what's really going on. Not even Betsy? How has she done it? How has she lasted? I don't know how I would have survived this summer if I hadn't come here. If I hadn't found Tyler.

"It's not fair to Austin," Dad says, "to go around spreading his private business. He's just a kid—he's just . . ." His voice is all choked up, and now I wish I hadn't asked the question in the first place.

"I'm sorry," I say, my voice starting to waver. I should be there with them for this, not two thousand miles away.

"Oh, Emma. No, no, no. You have nothing to be sorry for. And you're going to have such a great time at Yellowstone. I can hardly wait to hear all about it." Mom again.

"Take lots of pictures," Dad says, his voice sounding close to normal.

"I will. What time are you picking Austin up tomorrow?"

"Three o'clock," Dad says. "Cape traffic on Saturday will be a real beast, though, so who knows what time we'll be back home. It might be easier to FaceTime on Sunday, now that I'm thinking about it. How about we plan on that, E?"

"In the morning?" With the time difference,

that probably makes sense. It's two hours later for them, and I don't mind getting up early. Especially for Austin.

"Sure," Mom says. "Nine o'clock your time, eleven ours? How does that sound?"

"Sounds good."

"We miss you, kiddo," Dad says.

"So much," Mom adds. "It's way too quiet here. I'm not ready to be an empty nester, that's for sure. I think we'll have to get a dog or something once you're off to college."

"*Once* I'm off to college? How about now? I want a dog!"

Dad laughs. "One thing at a time, E. One thing at a time. We've got plenty on our plates right now as it is."

I think about Dumbledore for a sec and how he's maybe sort of grown on me. "What about a cat?"

They're quiet for a second. "Let's talk about that once you're home," Mom says. "We'd better rustle something up for dinner. Say hi to Delia and the crew and send them our love. I'll text some updates tomorrow, but otherwise expect to hear from us bright and early Sunday morning, 'kay?"

"Okay."

"Love you, Emma," Dad says.

"Love you, too," I tell them, and then click to end the call.

I flip back to that picture I showed Tyler, that one of Austin from last summer. I zoom in on my brother's face, back before everything happened. Is that what he'll look like when I see him on Sunday? Or will he look like the Austin I last saw, the one Dad had to practically babysit?

No. I shake my head, willing that image away.

He'll be back to how he used to be. He's better now. He promised.

Later that night, after I've finished the buffalo book, I tidy up the den. While we're at Yellowstone, a cat sitter will come by to take care of Dumbledore, but I do not trust that cat around my Becca box. I make sure to stash all the stuff I've collected from Goodwill and yard sales in a few file boxes in the closet. I put the Becca box on the highest shelf. Dumbledore is too fat to jump that high. It'll be safe.

At this point it's about 75 percent complete, but

that's okay because I've still got another three weeks to work on it after Yellowstone. Plus, whenever I'm working on a shadow box, time away seems to help. With a weeklong break from working on it, maybe I'll come up with some new ideas I wouldn't otherwise have if I'd kept working on it every day.

Before he left earlier today, Tyler gave me his grandmother's cell phone number, so we can stay in touch. He says I *have* to send him pictures of any and all buffalo I see. Easy.

When we get to the park the following day, it's late afternoon. All four of us are sick of being cooped up in the car. Since we're spending the first night at the Old Faithful Inn, Chris suggests we start with the park's most famous attraction.

Visitors are required to stay a ways back from Old Faithful. Too close and you'll get sprayed, Brian the park ranger tells us. And you do *not* want to get sprayed by boiling-hot water.

Point taken.

Brian's wearing one of those cool ranger hats. Well,

maybe not *cool* cool, but still, they're special. You can't get those hats just anywhere.

I'll be honest: it's hard to believe anything substantial is about to burst out over there. White smoke puffs out of a hole in the ground, but not much more than you'd see from a campfire. Is Brian *sure* this thing's going to spew scalding water more than a hundred feet into the air?

A little spurt shoots up, and an older woman with curly white hair and a cowboy hat in front of me yelps. Her husband shushes her. "That's not the real thing, Sally. We've still got another minute."

A moment ago Brian gave the forty of us gathered here his whole spiel about Old Faithful. Sadie could barely put down her phone to listen, but I did. On the drive out, Chris said people travel from all over the world to see Old Faithful, and it's one of his and Delia's favorite attractions in all of Yellowstone.

I'm not so sure yet. What can top seeing bison everywhere for the next few days? But I'm trying to keep an open mind.

I adjust my Red Sox cap and check my shoulders

for sunburn, and then all of a sudden there's less smoke pouring out and I know it's about to happen. I mean, true, Brian did tell us the whole reason it's called Old Faithful in the first place is because it's so predictable. But it's another thing to wait all this time, watching, watching, watching. Water begins spewing out—but not hundreds of feet yet, more like that splash park my parents took me to when I was little.

But then it's shooting up into the air. The thickest blast of water I've ever seen, spraying several stories high into the sky. "Now, *that's* an eruption," Chris says. Everyone gathered around us lets out a cheer.

I can't take my eyes off it. Not even for a second. The shock of white against the crisp blue sky. Smoke—or maybe it's actually mist—wafts off it, eventually evaporating.

Old Faithful continues to spray, though no longer to the highest heights, and then it slowly lowers until only the smoke remains.

Delia twists the top off her water bottle and takes a swig from it. "Wasn't that something?" She offers me some water, but I pass.

The thing is, it was. Words can't capture it,

exactly. How something can simmer under the surface like that, only the faintest trace of it, and then explode.

Sure, we can predict it now. Scientists studied it so we'd know all about how it works and why.

But how weird—how strange, unsettling, terrifying, really—must it have been to see it for the first time. To not understand what the smoke was signaling. To not know the rhythms. To watch something so ferocious explode right out of the earth.

By the time we're checking in to the Old Faithful Inn, my stomach is growling for dinner. Chris hands me and Sadie keys for the room we'll share the first two nights before moving on to explore other parts of the park.

As we head up the staircase, it's like I've stepped back in time to the early twentieth century. Hand-carved wood covers every inch of the place. A hundred years ago there was probably some woman in a hoop skirt grabbing the same gnarled railing I am now. "This place is amazing," I say to Sadie.

Sadie shrugs, but then, I'm not sure how much of

the place she's really seen, given how she's been glued to her phone the whole day.

We enter our room, and Sadie shuts the door behind us with a triumphant thump. She drops her suitcase by the bed closest to the door while I head for the one under the window and set my duffel on the floor.

My phone buzzes with a text from my mom. About time! I've only been checking my phone all afternoon for updates. Finally home. Cape traffic was so bad we stopped for dinner after the bridge.

How's Austin? I type.

It feels like the dot-dot-dot is there forever, but finally the message from Mom comes through.

He seems good, she writes. Looking forward to FaceTime tomorrow. Pics? XO.

I send her a few shots I got of Old Faithful. Heading to dinner soon. See you tomorrow! Give Austin a hug from me.

Even though the long car ride here was exhausting, I've got this strange burst of energy right now. Not Sadie, though. She's stretched out on the bed with her eyes closed, taking a nap. We've got a half hour till our dinner reservation, so I grab my sketchbook and head out to the balcony that wraps around the whole upstairs like an indoor porch.

Wooden rocking chairs face the lobby below. I spot an empty one and settle in, waiting for Chris and Delia to pop out. The texture of the wood here is incredible: knotted and whorled. It would be amazing to get my hands on something this special for a box someday.

I sketch the lines and patterns for a while, but then my hand starts to ache and I walk over to the large window that faces Old Faithful. The crowd in the lookout area now is at least as big as it was not even an hour ago when we were there. It's smoking still, the mist wafting our way.

It's different, watching it without Brian this time. I no longer know exactly when it's going to go. There's even more anticipation. Will it gush now?

No.

How about now?

My fingers rub the edges of the sketchbook, flipping one way and then the other.

Until it blows.

CHAPTER TWENTY-SIX

I blink my eyes open in the dark room, wondering why I'm awake. It takes a few seconds to remember where I am. Across the way I can just make out the little Sadie-sized hump beneath the quilt.

Did my phone wake me? Could it have been Austin? Did he text me? I reach for where I left it on the nightstand, but there are no new messages—from Austin or anyone—only the time: 2:03 a.m.

Back home it's two hours later. Not quite morning, even for an early riser like Mom. I like to think of all of them tucked into their beds, like in that book Austin used to read me around Christmas when I was little. All those little mice, tucked into their little mouse beds, fast asleep.

I set my phone back on the bedside table and try to

be like one of those mice. I close my eyes. I flip onto my side.

I flip onto my other side, patting down the pillow.

I lie on my back.

I lie on my stomach.

I check my phone again—it's been more than half an hour. And the thing is, I don't feel tired at all. Not really.

I slip out of bed, careful not to make a sound that would wake Sadie. I try to unzip my backpack to get my sketchbook, but the zipping feels too loud, so I just take the whole thing into the hallway, easing the door shut behind me.

No one's in the rocking chairs now. No night owls, I guess, except for me. Well, me and the guy working the front desk. But to be honest he looks pretty zoned out as he stares into the computer screen, every now and then clicking the mouse.

I'm about to settle into a rocking chair and sketch for a bit when it hits me: how eerie Old Faithful must look under the light of the moon. With bare feet, I pad over to the window. For now all that's out there is stillness. No shock of white. If there's smoky mist wafting out of the geyser, I can't tell in the dark.

But then something breaks the stillness. Out of the corner of my eye I catch movement beneath the bright lights of the parking lot. Stumbling forward out of the shadows on spindly legs—a baby buffalo.

The guy at the front desk doesn't even look up as the automatic doors part with barely a sound, and then I'm outside. The night air is cool, the concrete scratchy on the soles of my feet.

It's calm outside. No bustling crowds of tourists now. Nothing to see but the starry night sky. There must be a million stars, twinkling up above me. More than I ever saw back home with the light of the city so close.

It's all alone, just standing there, the bright lights of the parking lot like a spotlight. Without its mom or its dad or its herd.

Kind of like me.

My eyes are still adjusting to the dark as I come to a stop several yards away from it. The buffalo turns its head toward me, staring back with big cow eyes, and it feels like the whole summer has been leading to this moment since the drive out to Wyoming.

"It's okay," I say softly. "It's okay, buddy. I'm not going to hurt you."

There's no reason for me to be afraid. I'm not about to be gored to death. He—or she—is too small to do any damage. Still, I'm cautious. The mom could be lurking out there somewhere in the dark, waiting to charge me.

Instinctively, I almost reach out, but stop myself when I remember what I read. Human contact can make buffalo moms reject their babies. I can't touch it. Can't get too close. I don't want to ruin its chance of getting accepted back into the herd.

I circle around, maintaining a safe distance while trying to see if it's hurt. The buffalo is holding its back leg kind of funny, but I can't tell if that's just how it's standing or if it's injured.

"Are you hurt?"

The buffalo cocks its head to the side. I've almost finished circling when it takes a step forward and I see his *you know*. Okay, he's definitely a boy.

A small boy. Seventy or eighty pounds? Maybe a little more? I don't know how buffalo carry their weight, but he's smaller than me, that much I can tell for sure. His fur looks soft. I can see how the wrong person might try to pet him, treat him like some kind of oversized stuffed animal.

"Hey," I say, still keeping a safe distance. I don't think he's going to charge me, especially if it turns out he's injured.

His big brown eyes look almost sad as he stares back at me. Can a buffalo feel sadness?

"Did you get separated from your mom and dad?"

No answer, of course.

"My mom and dad are far away, but yours are close by, I bet. I'll help you find them." *How, Emma?*

His nostrils flare as he takes in a breath, but his tail still hangs limp. He's not afraid of me.

Behind me, the inn's lobby is all lit up. I could go inside and have that guy at the front desk call the rangers. But what if the buffalo leaves in the meantime? What if this little guy's really lost and he wanders off? What if he wanders into a geyser?

I pull out my phone, thankful for the internet even if it is just LTE, and search for the number for the front desk. Will anyone even answer the phone in the middle of the night?

"Old Faithful Inn—"

"Hello?"

"Yes?"

"Sorry—I'm staying at the inn. I'm outside in the parking lot and there's a baby buffalo. I think he's hurt. Can you radio one of the rangers? I don't want anything to happen to him."

"You say you're right outside?"

"Yeah."

"Let me put you on hold."

"He's going to help," I tell the buffalo. "I think. Well, I hope."

The automatic door slides open and the man from the front desk walks toward me. "Let's see what's up with this dude." He approaches the buffalo.

"Don't get too close," I warn him. "I think he might be hurt. And he's separated from his parents."

"Happens every now and then," he says, "especially in the more populated areas of the park. Let me radio the ranger station and see if they can send someone over." He removes the walkie-talkie from his hip, speaks some code into it, and waits for a response. "Pretty late to be outside."

"I couldn't sleep."

"You're not . . . going anywhere?" He gestures to my backpack.

"You mean, like, running away?" I laugh. "No. All I've got in here is my sketchbook."

"So you're an artist, huh?"

"Yeah," I say.

Static and then another voice blares from the walkie-talkie. He gives her our location. "Look, I've got to head back inside to cover the desk. You never know when someone in Singapore might want to make a reservation. A ranger should be over shortly." He reattaches his walkie-talkie. "You should probably be heading back to your room, given the hour and all. Wouldn't want your folks to think you'd gone missing."

I pat my pocket. "I have my phone. Plus, they're asleep. Can I just stay with him till the ranger gets here?"

He hesitates. "Well, I guess . . ."

"I'll let you know when I go back upstairs. So you'll know I didn't get kidnapped or gored to death." I smile.

"Deal." He offers up a fist bump, and we crash

knuckles. He walks back over to the inn, and then it's just me and the buffalo again.

He lifts up his nose a bit. Is he signaling something? I whip around fast, afraid his thousand-pound mom or dad might be behind me, lurking in the dark. But there's nothing there. Just a vast emptiness that goes on forever.

"Sorry," I say, my heartbeat slowing back down. "I'm not afraid of you. Promise."

We stand there in silence, each eyeing the other for several minutes until a ranger truck pulls in. A woman—her name tag says SUSAN—steps out.

"That was quick," I say.

"I was in the neighborhood. Now, let's take a look at this fella." She crouches down to examine the buffalo's back leg. "Poor kid got hit by something."

"A car?" A lump swells in my throat.

"Oh, he'll be all right. Not to worry. I'll radio one of our vets." As she pulls out her walkie-talkie, I lock eyes with the buffalo once more. Our time together is almost over.

Susan clips the walkie-talkie back to her waist. "You did the right thing, letting us know. Had this family last week, they treated the animals like they were the family dog. This fella might be small, but he's far from domesticated."

"They're beautiful," I say.

"They are something else, aren't they?"

"You have the best job. Living out here, seeing buffalo every day like this."

"Eh, you obviously haven't been here through the winter."

"True." But I've seen postcards of herds roaming across the snow-covered plains, geysers spraying into the harsh, cold air. It must be even more beautiful then, if a little lonely.

"Think we'll be forever making amends after what we did to them. Buffalo used to roam these plains by the million. How times have changed. Well, I've got things covered from here. Appreciate your help—sorry, what's your name again?"

"Emma. Emma O'Malley."

She reaches out a hand. Her grip is firm, the skin tough and leathery. "Nice to meet you, Emma O'Malley. Sue Clarendon."

"He'll be okay?"

“He’ll be fine,” Sue says. “He’s a resilient one. I can see it in his eyes. Can’t you?”

“Yeah,” I reply. I wish I could take his picture, to remember him—remember this moment—forever. But it’s too dark, and the flash would only startle him. Maybe it’s better this way. I stare at him hard one last time, taking a picture in my mind.

“Bye, buddy.” I give him a little wave and head back to the inn.

As I pass through the lobby, I yell out, “Night!” to the receptionist and head up the stairs. When I sneak back into my room, Sadie’s still deep asleep.

I climb under the covers. With my eyes closed, I can still see him: the buffalo I helped save. It doesn’t fix all the mistakes I made, but it’s one thing, one thing I got right.

And then I really do sleep.

The next thing I know, there’s a hand on my shoulder gently shaking me awake. “Emma?” I crack open my eyes. Sadie’s bed is empty, the room sunny and bright. What time is it? Did I sleep in? Did I miss the FaceTime call from Austin?

Chris is fully dressed, holding out a cell phone to me. "It's your mom," he says, his voice breaking.

The picture of Austin that flashes in my head when I take the phone from him and press it to my ear isn't the one from last summer. It's Austin in the hallway, blasting his fist into the wall.

My mouth goes dry as I take the phone from Chris. "Mom?"

CHAPTER TWENTY-SEVEN

For the flight out of Jackson Hole, the seat next to me is empty. Not that I want to talk to some stranger right now. I text the one person I can trust with the truth: Austin overdosed, but the EMTs revived him in time. He's stable. Heading home.

My throat tightens as I text the last bit. Sorry I didn't get to say goodbye.

Any minute now I'll have to switch on airplane mode, but until then I stare at the screen, grateful Tyler gave me his number before we left for Yellowstone. Grateful for Tyler, period. But then the flight attendant says we're pulling back from the gate, and I have to turn airplane mode on before Tyler has a chance to respond.

A few minutes later we're up in the air, crossing

over the park on our way to Chicago, where I'll switch to a plane for Boston. Another two-and-a-half-hour flight, plus a twenty-minute drive, and then I'll be home. *Home.*

I stare out the window at acres and acres of grassy plains, the sharp angles of the mountains in the distance, and the one thing I've been looking forward to seeing most of all. A whole herd of them. Dozens upon dozens of bison.

That's what it used to look like—not just Yellowstone, but all of the plains. What did my book say? Sixty million.

Sixty million bison used to roam the plains, but by 1900 there were only six hundred. Sixty million to six hundred. They were almost wiped out completely by people who cared only about money, who were so greedy that they killed nearly all of them until they were practically extinct. Strong and fast and powerful, but that wasn't enough to keep them alive.

That scary headline I saw online comes back to me. "Opioids could kill nearly 500,000 in the US in the next decade." Hundreds. Of *thousands*.

Could Austin be one of them?

I form a fist with my hand and bring it to my mouth. *No, Emma.*

I'm not ready to go back home. I'm not. My box for Becca is on the whole other side of Wyoming, on the top shelf of a closet. And it's not even done. I didn't get the chance to finish it, never mind come up with something for the art contest.

I'm supposed to have another month.

But nothing is going like it's supposed to. Maybe it never does. Not with me, not with Austin, not with anybody. Rehab was supposed to fix him. It was supposed to help. So how could something go so wrong before he'd even been out twenty-four hours? On the phone this morning, Mom and Dad said they weren't even sure what Austin took or where he got his hands on it.

He was supposed to be strong. He *used to* be strong. Like the buffalo.

But I guess he's not anymore.

Or maybe he is. All of those bison, all of them, they were strong, too. But then I think about the buffalo last night and how fragile he was.

Can you be strong and weak at the same time?

It's Dad who meets me at baggage claim in Logan Airport, still dressed in his suit and tie like he came right from the station. He's typing something into his phone—he doesn't see me, isn't even looking. "Dad?"

His head jolts up. "Emma!"

I crash into him, burying my face in his chest. He smells like cologne. We've never been apart this long, and it hits me all at once how much I've missed him. Delia and Chris were no substitute for the real thing.

"Do you have a checked bag or—"

"Dad." He's not really doing this, is he? Acting like this was planned, like he was supposed to pick me up from the airport today. "Dad, how is he?"

When he looks back at me this time, the cheery Tony O'Malley from channel 7 weather strips away bit by bit until it's only Dad in front of me. Not just *my* dad. Mine and Austin's. And he pulls me close, patting my hair in the way that only Dad does, which is to say, he's totally messing up my hair. "Better than this morning," he says. His voice breaks on the last word. "Oh, Em."

"Is Mom with him? How is she?"

"She's . . . holding up. Do you need to grab something to eat? Do you want to swing by the house first?"

"I just want to see Austin. I need to see him."

Dad reaches for my duffel, but I shake him off. I'm twelve; I can carry it myself. And as we head to the parking garage, neither of us says what we're thinking. Where do we go from here?

A nurse is in Austin's room when we get to the hospital, so Dad and I linger in the hallway. Outside the door is a whiteboard with my brother's name in blue erasable marker. But they didn't spell his name correctly. They wrote "Austen" instead, like that author my ELA teacher always raved about. I consider wiping my finger on the board, correcting it, but someone must have walked off with the marker, and anyway, it's not like I want Austin to be in there. Maybe if I leave it up, some different person is in there instead of my brother.

But I know that's not true because I can hear Mom's voice as she asks the nurse questions. Dad's shoulders slump as he stares at the wall. He keeps taking his phone out of his pocket, checking it, and putting it back.

The nurse startles when she exits the room. "Tony?

Sorry, I didn't realize you were out here. You know you can come in, right?" The way she calls him Tony instead of Mr. O'Malley makes me think she knows him from the weather. That she's maybe even a fan.

"Oh, that's okay. My wife's got things covered." He presses a hand to my back. "This is our daughter, Emma."

She shakes my hand. "Holly," she says. "Nice to meet you, Emma."

"You too," I say, even though it's not nice at all, actually. Does she forget why we're here? It's not like my imaginary big sister had a baby. We're here because Austin overdosed. He was supposed to get better. That's what thirty days on Cape Cod was all about. That expensive rehab facility Mom and Dad made five billion phone calls to get him into, it was supposed to fix him.

But it didn't. And now I'm not sure what will.

When we enter the room, Mom leaps up from the chair beside the hospital bed and hugs me tightly. "Em." A tear slips out of my eye, but I'm still pressed against her and it melts into her linen sweater. I'm the first to pull away.

Is it weird that I haven't even looked at him yet? My brother, tucked into blankets, attached to wires, connected to a machine that monitors—at least, I think—his heart. Jagged green lines and red numbers on a screen. I don't know what they mean, though I bet if I ask Mom or Dad, they'll tell me. That's my brother—that's Austin under those blankets with his head turned away from me. Sleeping. Just sleeping. Still alive.

A lump forms in my throat as I rewind, back, back, back, all the way to the fall, before everything changed. Austin's hand wrapped around the brown leather of a football, his fingertips on the white stitches. The cool air, the crunch of dead leaves. Becca and Kennedy and Lucy next to me in the stands.

We both made mistakes this year. Me and Austin. And we didn't tell each other about them the way we used to. The secrets we'd share when we were younger, stuff we'd never tell Mom or Dad. That time Austin broke the garage window and confessed only to me after swearing to Dad that he had no idea how it happened. That time I cheated on a spelling test in second grade and felt so guilty I had to tell someone, so I told him. We kept them for each other, the secrets.

And maybe that's why he couldn't tell me this time. This mistake was so big, too big for anyone else to keep secret. So he kept it all to himself.

But now we're here. In this too-cold hospital room on a late July night.

Someone has to say something eventually, so it might as well be me. "It wasn't fair," I say. Not to Austin, but to my parents. "It wasn't fair for you to send me away. You took it for granted that I—"

"I know," Mom says. "It wasn't fair to punish you. You hadn't done anything wrong. I'm sorry, Emma. If we could do it all over again, I—"

"No!" I can't let her keep thinking that somehow *I* was the good kid and Austin was the bad one. It wasn't that way at all. There's no such thing as the good kid. No one is ever all good, not me, not Mom, not Dad, not Tyler or Becca, not anyone. "Stop saying that."

"Saying what?" Mom asks.

"That I didn't do anything wrong. I *did.* You just don't know about it."

Dad cuts in. "What are you talking about, E?"

"What happened at Camp McSweeney with Becca. That night in the cabin. She—I—I ruined it. I totally betrayed her."

"Em, honey, slow down." Mom hands me a tissue from her purse, but it's not enough. I blow right through it, snot all over my hands, not that I care. Snotty hands are the least of my problems. "It's okay."

But it's not. Nothing's okay. I'm melting down. Austin's lying there asleep. Dad looks like a truck drove over him in the night. I sit down at the edge of Austin's bed to catch my breath, and when I finally do, I tell them everything. How it felt with Kennedy and Lucy. That's what friends were supposed to be. People who *got* you in every possible way. I never thought that Kennedy would open her big mouth like that so the whole school would know about the kitty blanket. I didn't mean to be mean. But I was anyway.

I wasn't the good kid. Not even close.

And Austin? I'm his sister. I should've known something was wrong. That night he wouldn't tell me where he was going, I should've told Mom and Dad. Even if it would have made him mad at me. I should've done it anyway.

Dad stops me there. "Oh, E. Please don't blame yourself for what happened with Austin. We didn't know—none of us. And part of me believes even if he tried to tell us, we would've been in denial. None of what has happened with Austin is your fault."

"Your dad's right," Mom says. "About Austin. That's on us. And, honey, I know you feel guilty for what happened with Becca on the trip, but from the way you told it at least, it sounds like Kennedy shares in the blame." Mom manages to find another tissue in her purse, and I use it to wipe up my hands. "You know, Dad and I expected you to be a bit more resistant about going to Wyoming. Now it's starting to make sense."

"Have you seen her—Becca?"

Mom shakes her head. "Between everything with Austin and the store, I haven't had much free time. Honestly, I'm so lost in my own head, for all I know I walked right past Dr. Grossman at the grocery store without even noticing."

Something nudges me in the butt right then, and when I turn around, Austin is lifting his head up off the pillow. His eyes flutter open and latch on to mine.

He keeps blinking like he's not sure I'm really here.

"Hey," I say, pivoting my whole body so I'm facing him.

"You came back."

I slide off the bed, taking a few careful steps toward my brother like I'm in one of those stores with breakable pottery.

He looks better than the last time I saw him. Clean-shaven. Healthy. Even though he's in the hospital. It doesn't add up.

His eyes get glassy, and he scrunches up his whole face. "I ruined your trip."

Was that how he still saw it? My *trip*? He didn't get it. Or maybe—maybe he did. Because he looks upset, finally, for all the pain he's caused. "You didn't ruin it," I say, surprised by how much that feels true. In spite of the circumstances, I had a great summer in Wyoming. Well, until now.

But I needed to come home. I needed to see him.

"It was my choice to come home," I say.

Maybe it wasn't only that Austin took me for granted. I took it for granted too, having a brother like him. The kind of brother he was before drugs got in the way and messed everything up. That wasn't the real Austin, the past six months. But this Austin, the one lying on the bed right now in front of me, that's *my brother.*

I rest my hand on his bed. The blue hospital blanket is covered in tiny fuzzy nubs.

"Did you make it out to Yellowstone yet?"

I don't tell him I only got to spend barely a day there. I just nod, rubbing a little blue nubby between my fingers.

"You get to see a buffalo up close?"

"I did," I say. I tell him about last night, how I stayed with that baby buffalo until I knew he'd be okay.

What I don't say, what I can't even try to without bawling all over again, is how I wish I could do the same with him. Just stay there and protect him, not let him do anything that could hurt him. Just stay there forever, keeping watch.

Austin drifts off to sleep again. "The drug they gave him this morning left him a little groggy," Mom says. "Takes a while to wear off."

I sit back down on the bed, taking care not to squish Austin's feet. "What happens now?"

"They'll be releasing him tomorrow morning," Mom says.

"To us?"

She nods slowly. "And then we'll try something different. One thing I've learned from the support group is that abstinence-only isn't the best path forward for most people. Medication-assisted treatment is."

"What does that mean, though?"

"Austin would be taking a medication and getting regular counseling—"

"He'd still be taking drugs? But isn't that what we're trying to fix?"

"Yes, Emma," Dad says. "To both. Substance use disorder, it's a disease. A complicated one. I know it doesn't always look that way, but we have to remind ourselves that. And educate others. This is no different than Austin having cancer or diabetes. And it might take several attempts to achieve remission." He reaches over and gives my hand a squeeze.

"I know you wanted to believe that after this first stint at rehab, everything would get better," Mom says. "Dad and I did, too. But the hard part comes now. And we can only take it day by day. All of us. Especially Austin."

Dad steps in. "What Mom and I are trying to say, E, is that this hard work is Austin's. It's not your job to watch over him. If that's anyone's job, it's ours. We're the parents. But we can't go back in time. All we can do now is provide our love and support, and be honest with each other. We're learning on the fly now. All of us."

I glance over at Austin, his chest rising and falling with each breath. The green line of that machine he's hooked up to, bouncing around. Up, up, up, then down. Up, up, up, then down.

Suddenly the lack of sleep from last night hits me, and all I want is to crawl into my bed and sleep forever. I search Mom's and Dad's faces, wondering how much they've wanted to do that too. Just crawl into bed and never come out. But they're here instead. Because they love Austin that much.

"Can someone take me home?"

Mom and Dad wordlessly duke it out for a moment until Mom says, "Sure, Em. I'll take you."

Someone must have just washed the hospital floor because Mom's running sneakers squeak on the linoleum as we make our way to the elevator. It comes right away, and when the door closes behind us, I'm surprised by the calm I feel.

Maybe it's that I'm so tired. Maybe it's from telling Mom and Dad everything, finally. Maybe it's from seeing Austin with my own eyes after a month apart.

Or maybe it's this, what I know now—I can't turn Austin back into the person he used to be. Dad's right: we can't go back in time. Austin's sick. He has a disease.

But I can still fix things with Becca. We can go back to how we used to be. I need her now more than ever.

And I can still win her back. I have to.

CHAPTER TWENTY-EIGHT

Even though I'm exhausted, there's something I need to do, and if I have to stay up all night to finish, well, that's just how it has to be.

Sure, the Becca box back in Wyoming was going to be perfect. But Becca knows I'm far from perfect, and maybe a box that's honest about that is just as good as a perfect one. Maybe imperfect is even better.

I grab my sketchbook from my backpack and dig the boxes out from under the bed. Drag out anything—everything—that reminds me of Becca and all the things we used to do together. Playbills from musicals we saw in Boston with her parents. A photo of us on the Swan Boats after years of begging my parents to let us go on them by ourselves. Seashells from the summer before fourth grade, when Becca's family rented that house on Nantucket and I got to tag along. All the small moments and memories—years of them.

I dig through my closet for the right box, and it's surprisingly easy to find. The box from the gift Becca brought back from Paris. The last gift she gave me before I messed up everything.

My hands are covered in glue, my floor a patchwork of cut-up photographs and magazine clippings, when there's a knock on my door. "You're still up?"

"I couldn't sleep," I say. Not that I was trying, but it's technically true. I can't. Not when I still need to make things right with Becca.

Mom lets herself in, stepping across the few bare spots on the floor until she's on my bed, sitting criss-cross applesauce. "What are you making?"

"A box for Becca. I'd started one back in Wyoming, but by the time they get back from Yellowstone to mail it to me—I can't wait. I just . . . I can't."

Mom reaches down and grabs a photograph of me and Becca from when we were in first grade. She and Dr. Grossman had enrolled us in dance class. We were little bunnies, with pink paint on our noses. We were supposed to be cute, I guess, except no one gave Becca the memo and in this picture she has the worst death stare ever. At the recital Becca tripped, knocking over me and three other girls and one boy. Yeah, that was the last time we ever took dance. (Probably for the best.)

"Oh, you girls were so sweet then."

I grab a photo of me, Becca, and Austin at a Red Sox game last summer, a candid Dad must have taken when none of us were paying attention. And I see it, for the first time maybe, how Becca looked at Austin like he was so much more than her BFF's older brother. Was that why she could never tell me who she liked? Because she liked *my brother*?

"I should've done this more," Mom says. "Peeked in on what you and Austin were up to. I always wanted to give you privacy—something I never had sharing a room with two sisters. But if I had, if I'd just kept closer tabs . . ."

"Mom, it's okay."

"No, it's not, Em. It's really not." She hands the photo back to me. "There was something you said earlier, about Kennedy and Lucy. Something I can't get out of my head. That they *got* you. Do you think Dad and I, that we don't?"

"Of course not," I say. But it comes out too fast. I set down the scissors and glance up at her. "Maybe a little?"

"Oh, Em."

"It's not your fault or anything. Just . . . you and Dad and A, you're all kind of the same. You like the spotlight. You like being around a ton of people. That's just not me, not who I am."

Mom reaches down for a photo of me wearing a crown made of flowers. That would be a normal cute picture of a three-year-old, but no, I had also painted my own face. Messy black-and-white stripes, like a zebra.

"You have been your own person from the first moment I laid eyes on you. I'm sorry it hasn't felt that way, and I will do better, but believe me, I see you, Emma. Every day. The beautiful person you're becoming." Mom wipes at her eyes, and I hate that I made her cry again today, after everything. But maybe this kind of crying is different.

"What I said before—about you being a good

kid . . . I don't expect you to always be good. I don't expect that you won't make mistakes. You and Austin, both of you are good kids, hon. Your goodness always outweighs your mistakes. I wouldn't want anyone else as my kids."

I spray some glue and sprinkle glitter over all of it. A tiny dusting so that the whole box sparkles, and then I hold it up to show Mom.

"Beautiful," she says.

"Can you sleep in here tonight?" I ask her.

Mom nods, already pulling back my sheets, and I see in her eyes how far she is past the point of exhaustion. "The mess can wait till the morning."

And she's right.

CHAPTER TWENTY-NINE

The brick walkway is exactly how I remember it, right down to the loose brick I once tripped over, skinning the bottom of my chin. Yeah, that was a *real* good look to start fifth grade.

Becca's house is one of the largest on the block, but it never felt as tall as it does to me this morning as I stand on the front step, reaching up for the brass knocker and holding her shadow box with my other hand.

Sure, I could've called first. That's what the old Emma would have done. *Knock, knock, knock.* I hear footsteps inside. Someone's coming. Will be here any second now.

I think about how it felt on the other side, back in Wyoming. That feeling someone had come over to see me, unannounced. *Me?* Really? Are you sure? Each time Tyler's face appeared on Delia's doorstep, that was how it felt.

It never got old, knowing someone was going to show up, actually be there for me, no matter what.

That was the person Becca used to be for me. She was always there. Always. Even when I tried to push her away. Now I need to be that person for her.

The door opens, but instead of Becca, it's her Bubbe, with her same curly gray hair and huge pearl earrings. She smells like cinnamon challah French toast. "Emma!" she exclaims. "It's been so long since I last saw you. Rebecca didn't mention you were coming. Are you joining us for breakfast?"

There's laughter in the background. Off to the side in the back of the living room, I see them. Four girls still in their pajamas, sleeping bags spread out on the floor. But I don't recognize any of them from school. Are they friends she made at camp?

Right behind Bubbe, coming down the stairs, is Becca. Her legs are right on the edge of sunburned and tanned. Her normally curly hair is straightened, and she's wearing a Harvard sweatshirt and pajama shorts, but not her glasses. Did she finally get contacts this summer?

Bubbe heads back to the kitchen, and Becca squeezes past her. "What are you doing here?"

"I . . . I . . ." I'm stammering, still holding the box. Do I give it to her now? What will she even do with it? Throw it in the trash? Show it to her new friends and laugh over it? Just Emma O'Malley and another one of her weirdo craft projects. "I'm . . ." But the "sorry" catches in my throat.

"Who is it?" one of the girls in the living room yells.

"Hurry up, Becs. You're going to miss the best part!"

Becca stares back at me, waiting for me to say something. Anything. And that's when I know, know for sure, that I'm too late. Maybe I had a chance if I'd thought of something like this back in June. But it says something—says a lot, actually—to not reach out at all. To leave town entirely for a whole month, never even saying where you're going.

I abandoned her. Not just once, but again and again and again.

She holds up one finger and then closes the door softly in my face.

CHAPTER THIRTY

I stand there a second longer, not entirely believing what just happened. And then it sinks in.

As I'm fleeing Becca's house, I trip on that loose brick, tumbling to the ground like a little kid. As I'm going down, I let out a yelp, but nobody comes to save me. The shadow box cushions my fall, but my body crushes the shadow box and it's ruined, just that fast.

You can build something beautiful—a shadow box, a life—and squash it in an instant.

I pick myself up off the ground. My knee isn't scraped too bad, but the palm of my hand sure is from trying to stop the fall. Tiny bits of gravel are pressed into my skin, and there's a light sheen of blood coating my whole palm. I press it to my shirt, but that only makes it sting worse.

I walk down Becca's driveway, bloody palm prints on my pale gray shirt. I glance back, sure someone has to be watching this in a window. Becca and her new friends, laughing at me. But there's nobody in the window, only curtains.

I make it to the shady spot beneath the magnolia tree where Becca's driveway meets up with the sidewalk and dump the smashed shadow box in the trash bin, and that's when I lose it. The ugliest of ugly cries. Huge sobs rise up in my chest, and I can't swallow them back down.

This thing with Becca—I can't fix it. I was stupid to think I still could. Too much time has passed, and she doesn't want anything to do with me. And the worst part is that it makes sense. Why would she come crawling back to me after how I treated her? She's not dumb. Of course she'd move on. Of course she'd find new friends, find her people at Harvard. Of course.

A woman pushing a jogging stroller barrels down the street right past me. She doesn't even stop to ask why I'm all bloody or try to help. It's like I'm invisible again, like back at the beginning of sixth grade. How quickly I forgot that feeling.

I reach into the pocket of my shorts for my phone, my palm stinging against the denim. I'm about to call Tyler when I hear something. It sounds like my name, but it can't be.

"Emma, wait!"

It's Becca, her flip-flops slapping on the sidewalk as she jogs to catch up with me. "I closed the door to tell them I'd be right back, and then you were gone and—oh my gosh, Emma, what happened? Your shirt. Your—your hand."

"I tripped."

"On that brick again?"

She remembers. Of course she does. "You should really get that fixed," I say with a laugh.

"You're the only one who ever tripped on it. We always go in through the garage." We're both walking in step now, though I don't know where we're going. "Why did you come over? I haven't seen you since school let out. I was starting to think you'd vanished."

"I've been in Wyoming."

"Wyoming?"

I don't get it—how we're having a normal conversation right now, almost as if nothing happened, when something did happen. And that something was all my fault. "Aren't you still mad at me?"

Becca goes quiet for a second. Old Becca probably would've adjusted her glasses or something, but this new Becca doesn't have them anymore. I wonder what else has changed. A month seems like such a short time, but it can be a long time too. "A little," she says. "I mean, I was really mad about what happened at Camp McSweeney—"

"Becca, I'm so sorry. I'm so, so, so sorry." My eyes are smarting again. "I made you this special shadow box—back in Wyoming—to show you how sorry I am, but then I didn't get to finish it. And then I made one last night after I got back, but then when I tripped, I smashed it. I ruined it. I—"

"It's okay, Em. It's okay. I mean, it was weird at first. I thought I'd hear from you sooner, but then, things have been kind of weird between us for a while, right? Ever since you started hanging out with Kennedy and Lucy. Maybe even before."

She's not wrong.

"I didn't get it then. I was jealous. But now, now I think I get it."

"Get what?"

"I hadn't met anyone before that I really clicked with, but then at camp this summer, I made these new friends and it was different. Easy. Not that being your friend was hard—it's just . . . we didn't fit together the same way, like how we used to. Sometimes you meet someone and it just makes sense."

"Like me and Tyler."

"Wait, did you get a boyfriend this summer?"

"No, no," I say, laughing at the idea. "He's a friend I made in Wyoming. Becca?"

"Yeah?"

I know Mom and Dad haven't given me the all clear yet to tell people what's going on with Austin, but I know they trust Becca. And after what happened with Austin, chances are they aren't going to be able to keep this a secret much longer.

"Austin's sick."

We're still walking, but Becca's steps have halved in length. "With what?"

I fill her in on all that's happened between the shoulder surgery and now as we make a big loop around our neighborhood. Maybe Becca and I don't quite click anymore when it comes to a lot of stuff, but when it comes to Austin, we still do.

"You must be so worried about him," she says.

"I am." I don't know when the worry will ever stop, only that it feels so good to tell Becca about it.

We're almost back at her house now. I know I can't keep her out here forever. She's got friends waiting inside.

"Becca?"

"Yeah?"

"Can we just—"

When you've been friends since you were four, there are some things you can say without speaking a single word. And as we wrap our arms around each other, I know it's not the last time, but also that we can't go back to the way things used to be. Our friendship has changed, but it doesn't mean we don't care about each other. It'll never mean that.

"You smell different," I say, and then laugh. "Not that you're smelly. It's just—your hair. Did you change shampoos?"

"It's the straightener," Becca says. "Do you like it?"

"It looks really pretty."

Becca scrunches her nose like she's not so sure. "I think I miss the curls. But it's not permanent, right?"

"Right," I say, and I smile.

Thankfully, few things are.

CHAPTER THIRTY-ONE

On the short walk back to my house, I call Tyler and update him on Austin and my makeup with Becca.

Mom's not back from the hospital with Austin yet, so I let myself in and head to the bathroom to wash off my hand.

"I'm putting you on speakerphone, okay? I've got to wash the blood off before Mom and Austin get home."

"Uh, Emma? The *blood*? Did you leave something out? Like, I don't know, a *murder*?"

I let out a laugh so big it sounds almost like an evil cackle. "Yes, Tyler. I murdered someone," I deadpan as I pull out the drawer where Mom keeps first aid supplies. "No! I tripped on Becca's front step, remember? Although, now with blood all over my shirt and shorts, it actually does a little bit look like I murdered someone."

"Can we switch to FaceTime? I need to see this."

I click to accept his FaceTime call and then hold back the phone to show him my murderer ensemble. Now that I think about it, I could use it for a pretty scary shadow box. Though I don't know if a murder box would have a shot at winning that contest. More likely it would lead to a call to the local police.

"It doesn't look *that* bad. Though I like your bathroom. Marble countertops? Fancy. Emily Gilmore would approve."

"Aw, we didn't get to finish our *Gilmore* binge." I wince, dabbing the cut on my hand with a rubbing-alcohol-soaked cotton ball.

"There's always next summer," Tyler says. "Maybe if I start doing some chores around the neighborhood, I can save up enough money for a plane ticket to Boston! I could mow lawns, walk dogs, feed cats—well, as long as they're nicer than Dumbledore."

"Or we could come to you." I slap a Band-Aid on my palm. It's hard to imagine a whole year out, especially when I'm trying to take things one day at a time.

But maybe next summer Austin will be doing better and we can fly out as a family. See the buffalo together.

"But then how am I going to get to see Stars Hollow?"

"Ty, it's not real."

"You know what I mean. New England! Ooh—sorry, Em. I've got to go in a sec. We're almost there."

"Almost where?" I ask, suddenly noticing that Tyler's been in a car this whole time.

"I'm with Grams. We're going to see my mom."

There. He means the prison. "When did you change your mind?" I head outside and sit on the front steps.

"When you texted me yesterday about Austin and heading home, it hit me. My mom's so far away. Anything could happen to her—stuff happens in prison, you know? And I don't want her to think I don't love her. It's not that I'm not mad at her still, but I love her too. That counts more."

What Mom said last night, about the goodness counting more than the mistakes, comes back to me. "I'm glad you're seeing her."

"Me too."

Just then Mom's Subaru Outback turns up our

block. "Hey, Ty? Mom and Austin are back. I've got to go. Text me later, 'kay?"

"I will."

"Emma, what happened?" Mom exclaims as I click out of my call with Tyler.

"Dude, you lose a fight with a bottle of ketchup?" Austin chuckles, and for a moment it feels like nothing has happened, that he's the same Austin he was a year ago. Even though I know that's not possible.

"I'm okay. I just—I tripped."

"Let me get some bacitracin for you," Mom says, squeezing past me to go inside.

"I already took care of it."

"You know, sometimes I forget how much you've grown up." Mom does that little smile and head tilt that makes me think she might cry.

"Mom, stop," I say, and she does. I head into the backyard. Austin follows me out to the couple of worn-out Adirondack chairs and sits down first. There's a football resting in one of them, and he picks it up and starts gently passing it from one hand to the other. "You going to tell me what happened?" He gestures to my shirt.

"Do you remember Becca's kitty blanket?"

"That ratty old thing? Yeah, what about it?"

And so I tell him. About what happened at Camp McSweeney, but also what happened before and after. How maybe my friendship with Becca is kind of like the kitty blanket. I still need it, even though it isn't everything it once was to me.

Maybe it isn't just that I was outgrowing Becca this year but that she was outgrowing me, too. This summer we both made new friends. Even if Tyler is two thousand miles away now, I know he's there for me, just like Delia is for my mom. And he gets it, everything that's going on with Austin. Probably more than Becca ever could.

"I hope people still aren't making fun of her when school starts." I pick at some flaky paint on the chair.

"You think people will still remember?" Austin leans back in the chair. With his longer hair, he doesn't look so much like star-quarterback Austin anymore. But he doesn't look like he has problems with drugs either. I guess there's a lot you can't tell just from looking at a person. "In September? Em, middle school moves waaaaay too fast for stuff like this. Trust me, it'll feel like a blip by the time you're back in school. Everyone will have moved on over the summer. There'll be five billion other things to care about."

"Really?" It's hard to imagine at first—all I can think of are those last few days at school and the endless meowing. But then I think about this summer and how much can change in just a month.

I don't know what I was thinking, imagining we could go back to the people we used to be. Like the buffalo. They came back from almost dying off, but it's not like things went back to the way they were before. They couldn't roam the plains anymore. There were too many people. The whole country had changed.

You can never really go back.

And even if I could, would I want to?

Would I really want to be the Emma who'd never been friends with Kennedy and Lucy? Who'd never met Tyler? The Emma who'd never traveled two thousand miles by herself and lived in Wyoming for the summer? The Emma who'd never saved a buffalo?

I don't want to be that Emma again, even if I could.

Is that true for Austin, too? Or does he want to go

back to before, even if it's impossible? There's so much I haven't asked my brother. So much I want to. All summer long, I couldn't. But now he's right here, in the chair next to me.

"Austin," I say.

"Yeah?"

"Why did you—" I start and stop. He's looking right at me. One hundred percent at me, like how he used to. "Sorry. It's just, I don't understand why you would do drugs. Your life before, it was perfect."

"Perfect?" He laughs, and then his eyes shift to something off in the distance. He sits there so still that for a second I think maybe I shouldn't have said it. Maybe after what happened the other day, it's too soon.

He chews on his lip, and I worry he's going to cry or lash out at me. Something. But he doesn't. He says, so plainly, "Nobody's life is perfect, Em. If there's one thing I learned at rehab, it is definitely that. But I don't know. . . . I don't think there's one why. At least for me. There are a lot of reasons, and I'm still—I guess I'm still untangling them. If that makes any sense."

Even though I'm not entirely sure what Austin's

saying, I nod. Because he's finally being honest with me. He's telling me his truth.

But maybe there are some truths you can't tell with only words.

"Hey, Austin?"

"Yeah?"

"I need to run inside and get something, but can you stay right here? I'll be right back. It'll only take a second."

"Sure, Em." He's still holding that football in his palms when I leave him to get my sketchbook.

I think I know what to make for that art contest.

* * *

WHERE WE USED TO ROAM

EMMA O'MALLEY

AGE: 12

MIXED MEDIA

When Delia and her family returned from Yellowstone, she mailed my stuff back to me. Three big boxes of the mess I'd left behind in my room: all the stuff Tyler and I had found and then some. And of course my Becca box.

The idea came together as I talked to Austin that morning in the backyard, and right away, I knew which box made the most sense. I found it in the entryway closet, way up at the top. The shoebox that used to hold Austin's football cleats.

Once my stuff arrived from Wyoming, on the inside of the box I glued pictures from those magazines Tyler and I had found at Goodwill: images of the plains and the beauty that once belonged to just the buffalo and the Native Americans. And in the center I tacked that portrait drawing I made last November in art class. The one of Austin.

I decoupaged the outside of the box with newspaper articles about the opioid epidemic. They weren't hard to find. The *Boston Globe* had at least one in every issue. I cut them out every day for the rest of the summer, the little stack growing taller and taller each week.

People were dying. Every day, somewhere, someone was dying.

But every day, people were getting better too. They were resilient. Coming back strong, like the buffalo. Maybe even stronger than they knew.

Like my brother.

Since the morning he was discharged from the

hospital, Austin went out for a run with Mom every day. They'd go for at least five miles, running on trails nearby or on the sidewalks through town. Sometimes if I was home, I'd tag along. Only for a mile or two though. And even then, I'd be all sweaty and out of breath by the end.

Austin said it helped, and of course Mom loved it. Running, her and Austin. Most of all, we were just happy to see Austin be Austin again. Maybe not the same Austin from before. I knew he'd never be exactly that Austin again, and that was okay.

The new Austin helped me with my homework and joined the cross-country team. He went to Narcotics Anonymous meetings and therapy and said he wasn't going to have a girlfriend for a while. He said he had a lot to figure out about himself first.

He hadn't relapsed yet. Sixty days, abstinent. Every day was a new day. Every day. For all of us.

I can't tell you how many times I tried to sketch that baby buffalo. Each time it failed to match up to the image in my head. I could still see him so well in there. Tyler was the one who suggested going to my public library to use their 3D printer. Only then did he become real again, exactly how I saw him. The buffalo I saved. Or, well, tried to. He was probably strong enough to save himself.

I glued him to the bottom of the box. Behind him I tacked several empty orange pill bottles, the same kind Mom found in Austin's room back in June.

"Emma?"

Her mouth full of cheese and crackers, Kennedy bounds over to me. Whoever set up this art show is taking us seriously with the snack spread. "Emma, it's incredible."

This summer at RISD she'd taken her drawing to a whole other level. Learned how to animate, so she wasn't only drawing manga now. She'd made a five-minute anime video for the contest.

"It's not as good as yours," I say.

"It's deeper," Lucy says. "No offense, Ken, but . . . you know what I mean."

Kennedy crunches on a cracker, examining my box from every angle. She flicks the white ribbon tacked up next to it. "Third place? Pssshh. The judges don't know what they're doing."

Her video had been awarded first place in its category, though to be fair, there weren't as many entries in video art as there were in mixed media. Lucy's gigantic self-portrait made out of plastic pushpins had won first place *and* best in show. I still can't wrap my mind around how she even thought of that—so brilliant, so Lucy.

We'd been back to school for two weeks now, though I'd opened the envelope the two of them mailed from RISD as soon as Delia sent it with all my stuff. Along with a bunch of drawings, Kennedy had written me a letter about how she felt so intimidated by Grace Collins and them that she just blurted it out. She wasn't thinking and she never meant to make things so hard for Becca. She'd reached out to Becca on her own and apologized. I probably would've known that if I hadn't waited so long to try to make things right myself.

And Lucy—get this—she wrote me about her stepsister Erin and how she still sleeps with her baby blanket even though she's married! And about this comedian guy, this tall, handsome grown-up, who talked about his baby blanket in his Netflix special.

"Do you want to walk around, check out the other pieces?" Kennedy asks. "Or get some snacks?" She reveals her empty napkin and makes a melodramatic sad face.

"Sure," I say, and we go over to the snack table to grab some grapes and Brie, like dignified artists. Well, until Kennedy tries to snag a grape branch and a bunch of loose ones end up rolling all over the floor.

As we're walking to the front of the room where the crowd has finally thinned out, I catch Mom and Dad talking with some parents of Austin's old friends from the football team. It's not a secret anymore. Once Austin was home, Dad started going to those meetings on the North Shore with Mom. They were worried at first about what it would mean going public. Would it affect business at Mom's store? Would people treat Dad differently at work?

But what happened was the opposite of what they feared. When the station ran a special on the opioid epidemic in greater Boston for National Recovery Month, Dad recorded the intro. Channel 7 even came and filmed a segment with him, Mom, and Austin in our living room. The response from viewers was overwhelming. So many people wrote in about how much it helped for him to put his name and Austin's story out there. Dad said if they could help just one person suffering in silence, as Austin had been, to get help, it was worth it.

Out of the corner of my eye, I catch her by my shadow box. Her hair is back to its usual curliness, and she's not wearing glasses. Her cable-knit sweater is tight, almost preppy-looking. I honestly wouldn't be entirely sure it was Becca if not for what she's holding in her right hand. Her security blanket. Well, the socially acceptable kind. A library book.

I barely see her in school—she's taking more classes at the high school this year.

I tap Lucy on the shoulder. "Be right back." And then I squeeze my way over, passing by Mom and Dad until I'm standing right beside her, staring at my shadow box.

"It's really good, Emma."

"Thanks," I say quietly.

"Don't you think the buffalo kinda looks like her?" Austin steps in beside us.

That quickly, Becca's cheeks go pink. *I knew it.*

"It *does not* look like me," I say, swatting him.

"What are you talking about? He's got your hunched back, your furry legs—sorry, Em, but it's probably time to shave those things."

"My back's not hunched!" He's probably right about my legs though. I think my blond hairs are starting to turn brown.

Austin hulks over, doing his best impression of me as a buffalo, and I'm borderline choking on a cracker.

Becca's laughing so hard she's crying, and people—perfect strangers in the gallery—are starting to stare at us.

We're all such a mess. Me. Austin. Even Becca.

It's funny how I ever thought I could contain a person in a box. Becca. Austin. Anyone. The thing about boxes: they have only so much space. A box can never fit everything about a person. Can never even come close.

All my shadow boxes ever really capture is me—how I see things in one particular brief and fleeting moment. They're like time capsules in a way. A gallery, really, of all my former selves. Because by the time I'm finished, I'm not that Emma anymore. I'm changing too.

I look at my brother, his eyes squinting as he laughs. Becca's crimson cheeks. The tiny buffalo behind them.

I wonder what I'll make next.

ACKNOWLEDGMENTS

Some books take winding and circuitous paths or are born from fragments of abandoned projects. *Where We Used to Roam* is both of these things. It was partly inspired by a YA work-in-progress set aside after I wrote *14 Hollow Road.* At points in the process of writing this book, it felt like everything that could change did. I am grateful for the many wise voices who chimed in along the way. First and foremost, I want to thank my agent, Katie Grimm, who read way more versions of this book than she ever should have had to, but who saw what it could be and helped me get it there, every step of the way. I am deeply appreciative of the guidance of my editors: Tricia Lin, for helping me fine-tune this story and keep the focus on Emma's journey, and Kristin Gilson, for taking it over the finish line. So many others provided essential feedback and encouragement: Anne Bowen, Abby Cooper, Kelly Dyksterhouse, Stephanie Farrow, Robin Kirk, Autumn Krause, Laurie Morrison, Aimee Payne, Jen Petro-Roy, Bonnie Pipkin, Ellen Reagan, C. M. Surrisi, Monique Vieu, and Matt Zakosek. Thanks also to Ambrose Cohen for his football acumen and the many doctors in my family who helped on the medical end: Kara Bischoff, Ben Hulley, and George Hulley. A huge thanks, as always, to my parents and my husband, for their unwavering support. And to my cat, Lilly, for being dangerously, distractingly cute.

When I first began researching and writing about the effects of a loved one's substance use disorder, the opioid epidemic was just starting to ravage northern New England. In the years since, it has only continued to rob so many of their lives, livelihoods, and loved ones across the country. Journalists at the *Boston Globe* and the *Cincinnati Enquirer* helped open not just my eyes, but the eyes of so many, and I'm ever grateful for the attention they continue to draw to this ongoing public health crisis. Other books that helped shape my understanding include *Dopesick: Dealers, Doctors, and the Drug Company that Addicted America* by Beth Macy, *Dreamland: The True Tale of America's Opiate Epidemic* by Sam Quinones, *Everything is Horrible and Wonderful: A Tragicomic Memoir of Genius, Heroin, Love, and Loss* by Stephanie Wittels Wachs, and *If You Love Me: A Mother's Journey Through Her Daughter's Opioid Addiction* by Maureen Cavanagh.

After my first year in college, I spent the summer in the northeastern corner of Wyoming with my best friend's family. I didn't save a buffalo like Emma—if only—but the landscape and people I met there have continued to shape my life. Thanks again to the Roosa family for all that you exposed this bison-crazed New Englander to and for your friendship over the years.